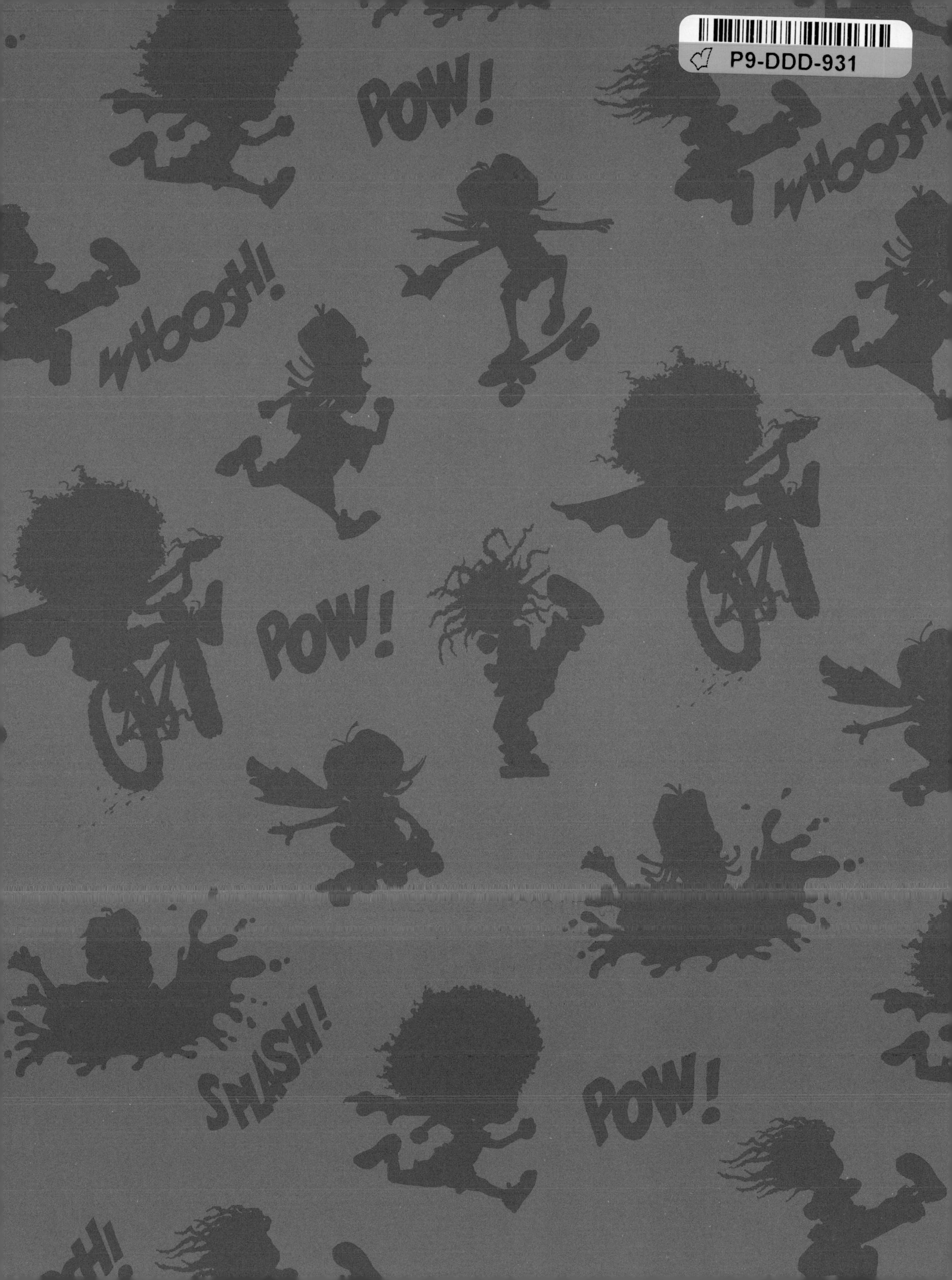
POW!
WHOOSH!
WHOOSH!
POW!
SMASH!
POW!

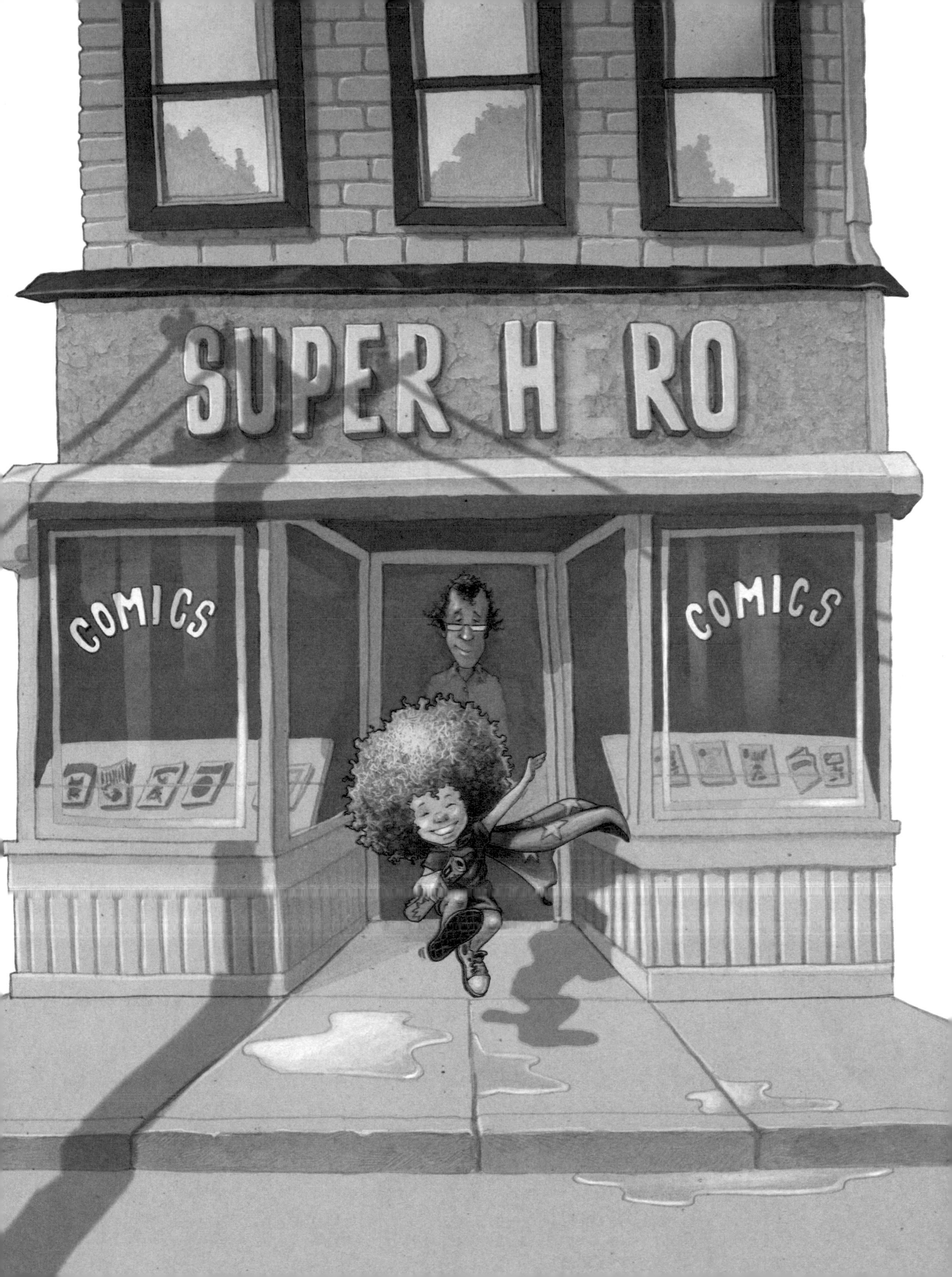
SUPER H RO
COMICS
COMICS

This book is for my mom

Copyright © 2013 by John Rocco
All rights reserved. Published by Disney•Hyperion Books, an imprint of
Disney Book Group. No part of this book may be reproduced or transmitted
in any form or by any means, electronic or mechanical, including
photocopying, recording, or by any information storage and retrieval
system, without written permission of the publisher. For information
address Disney•Hyperion Books, 114 Fifth Avenue, New York, New York
10011-5690.

First Edition
10 9 8 7 6 5 4 3 2 1
H106-9333-5-13046
Printed in Malaysia

Library of Congress Cataloging-in-Publication Data
Rocco, John.
    Super Hair-o and the barber of doom / by John Rocco.—1st ed.
        p.   cm.
    Summary: A boy fears that he has lost his superpowers after a villain
captures him and cuts the hair that he believes is the source of his strength.
ISBN 978-1-4231-2189-3
[1. Superheroes—Fiction. 2. Haircutting—Fiction.] I. Title.
    PZ7.R5818Sup 2013
    [E]—dc23   2012003842

Reinforced binding
Visit www.disneyhyperionbooks.com

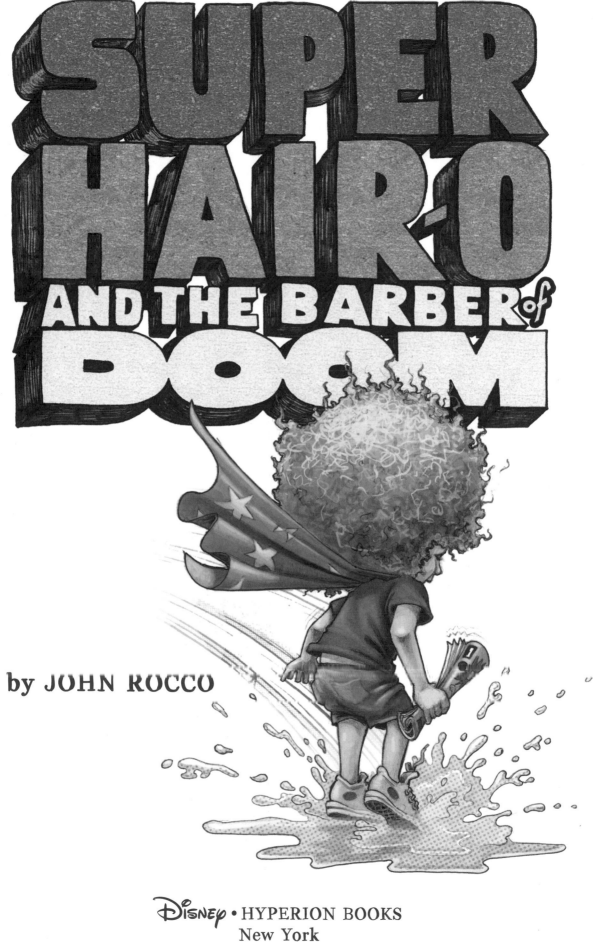

SUPER HAIR-O AND THE BARBER of DOOM

by JOHN ROCCO

DISNEY • HYPERION BOOKS
New York

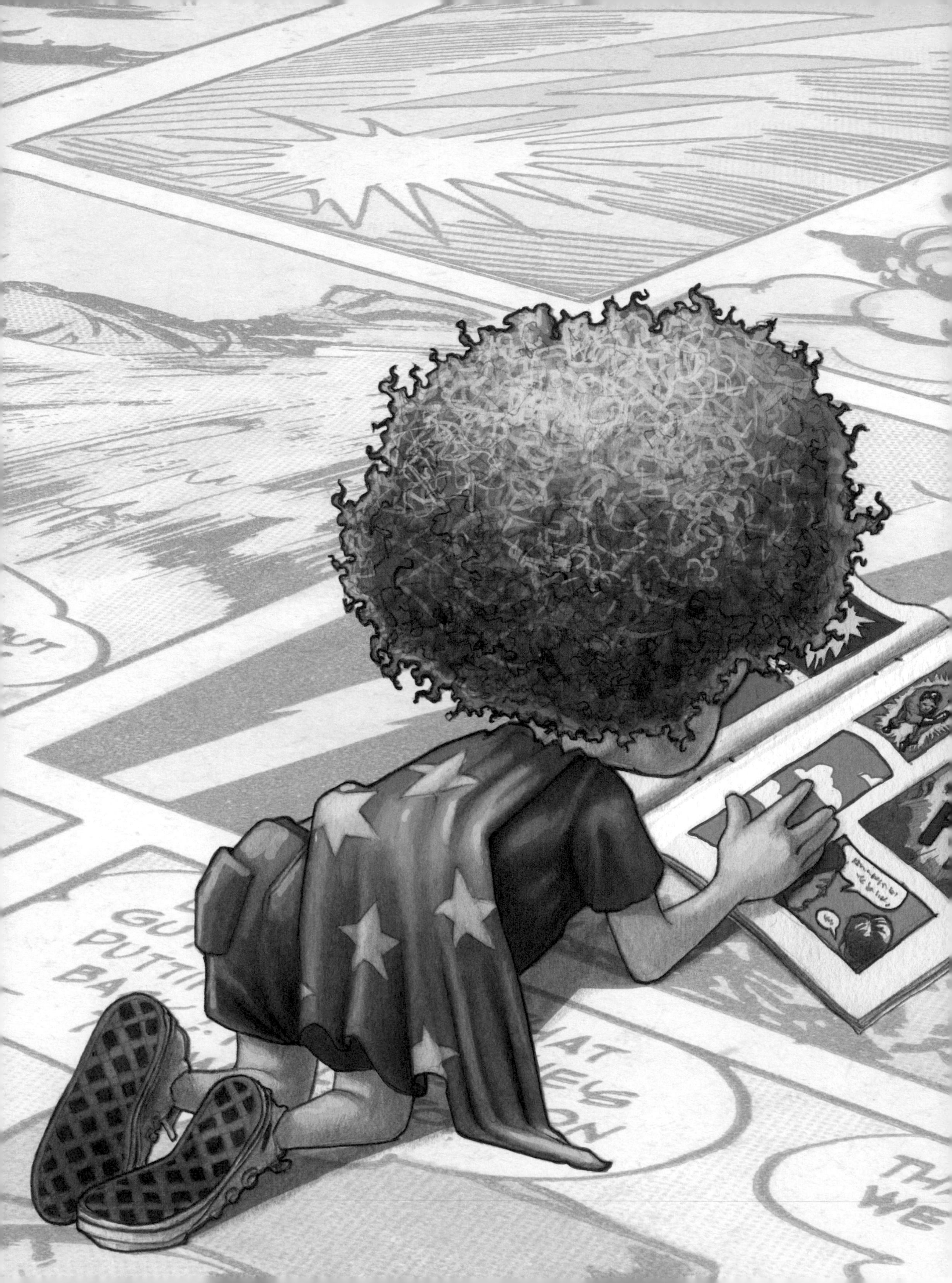

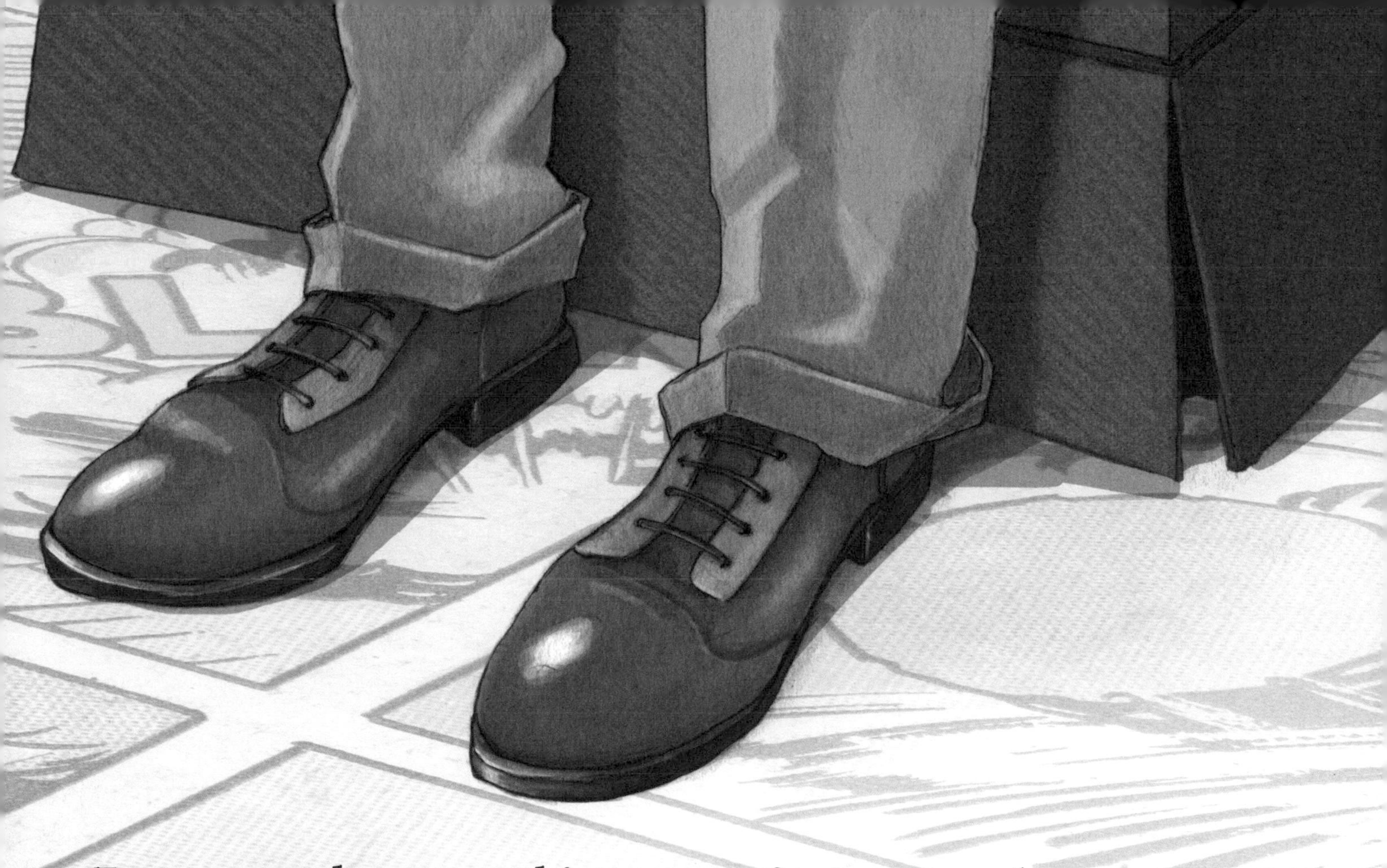

Every superhero gets his powers from somewhere. **Photon Man** had his ring. **Robo Girl** had her bionic arms. My **superpowers** came from my hair.

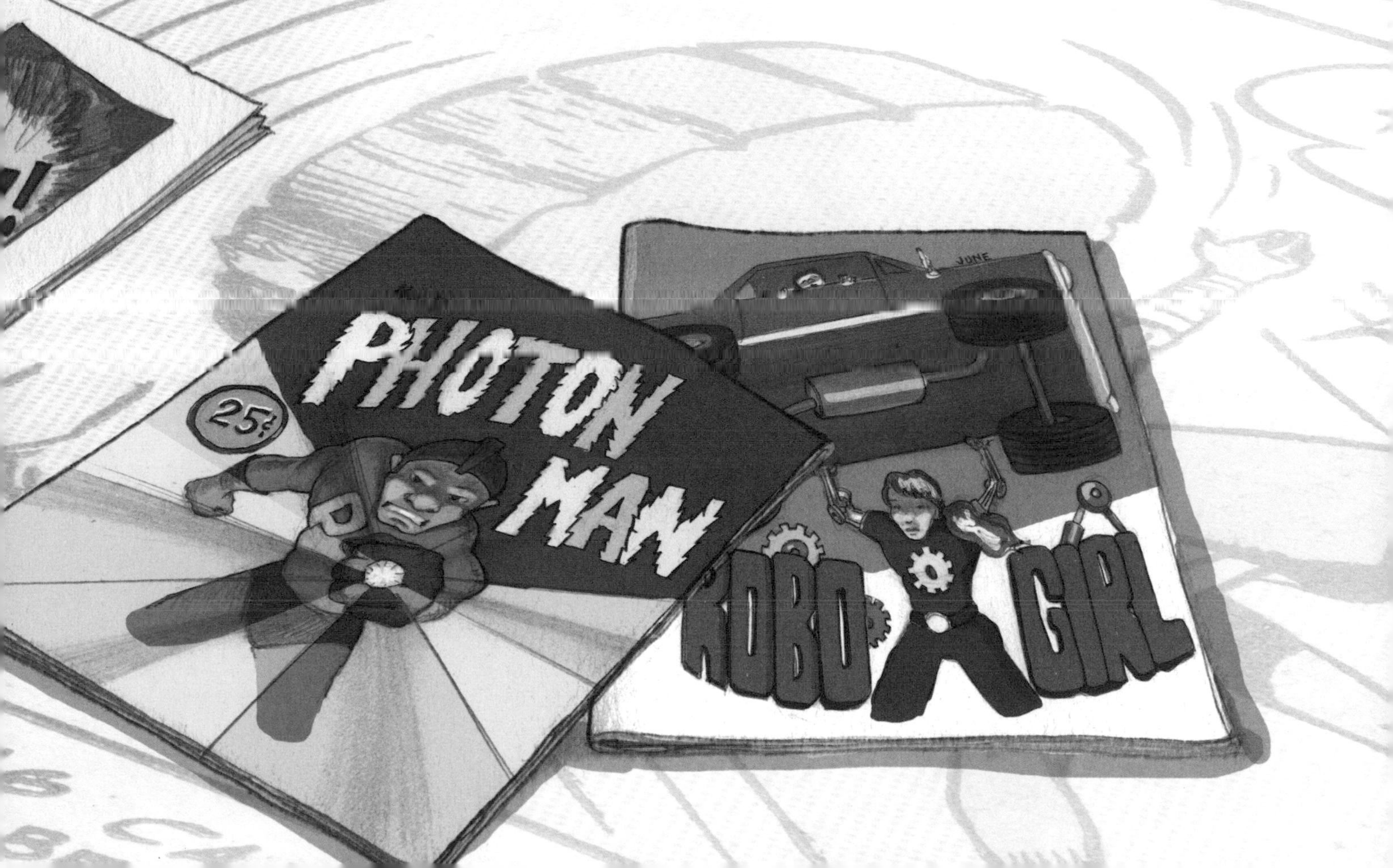
PHOTON MAN
25¢
JUNE
ROBO GIRL

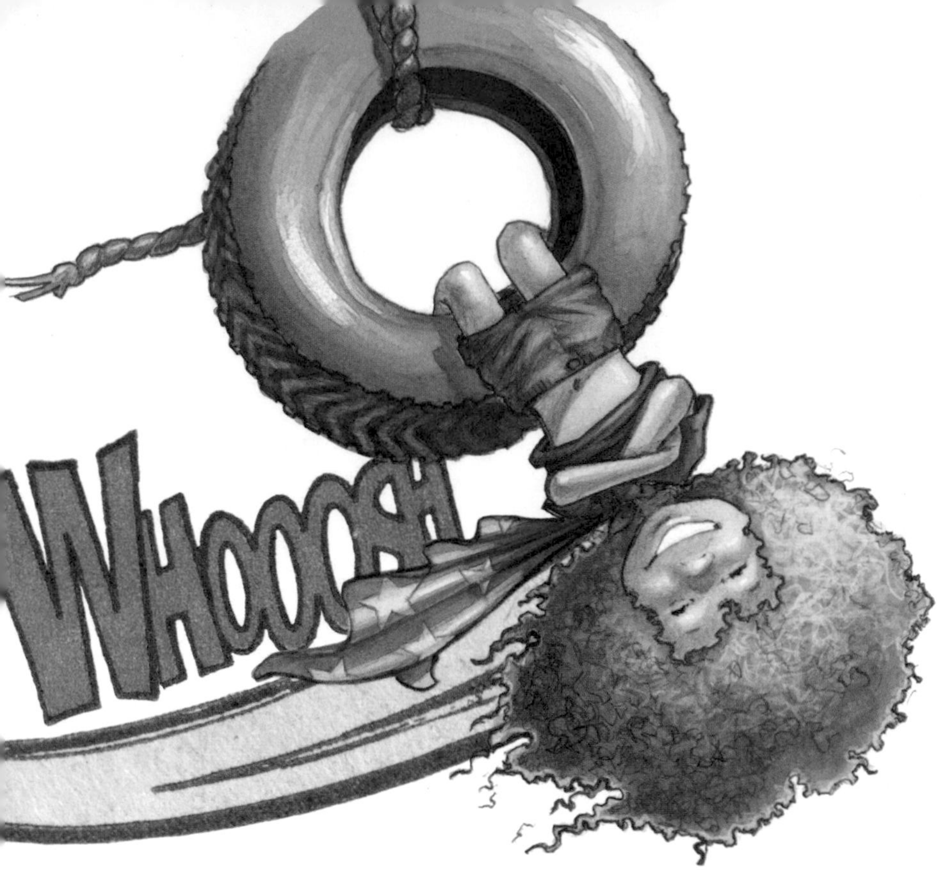
WHOOOSH

The more my hair grew,
the more **awesome** my superpowers became.

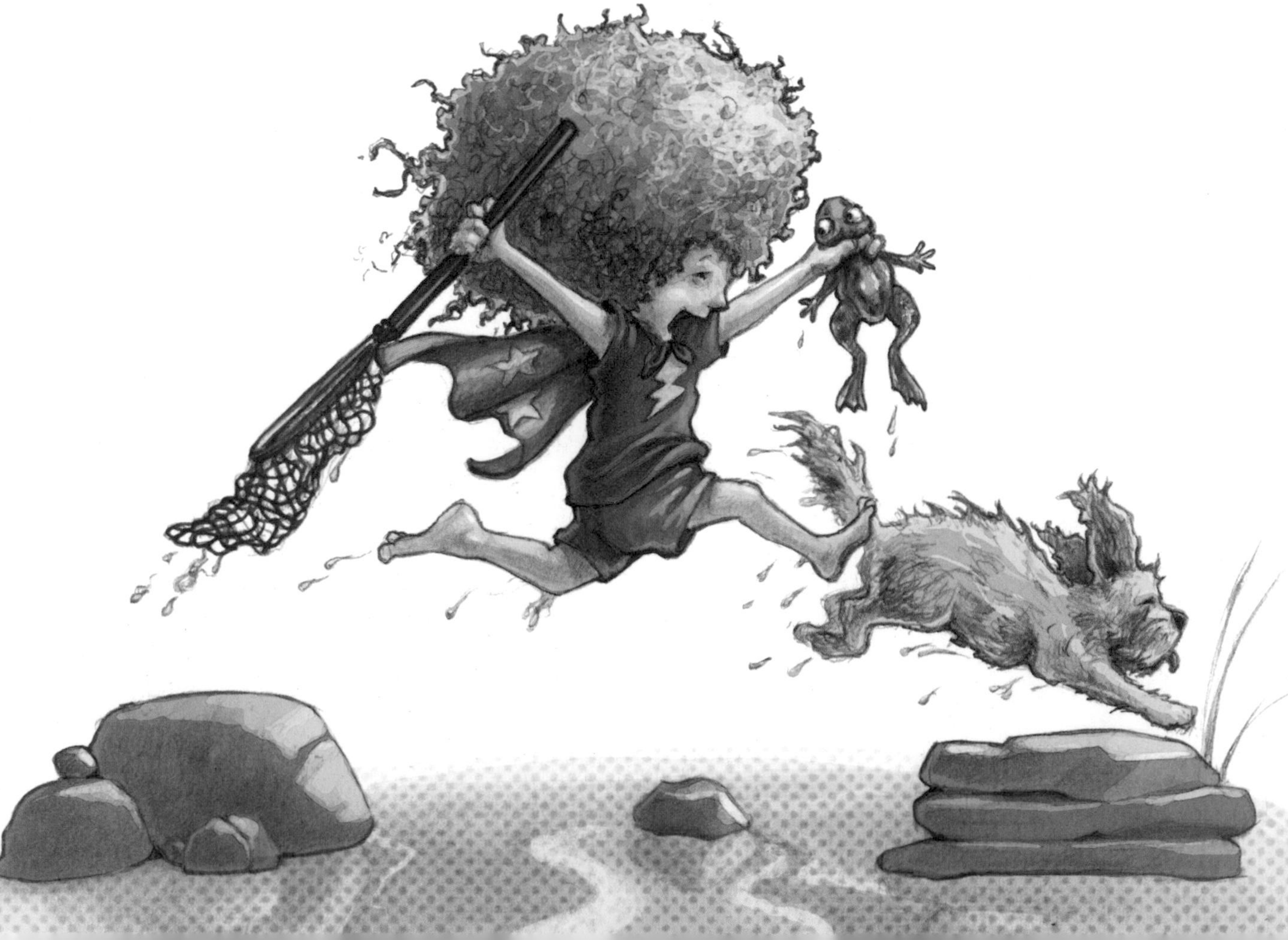

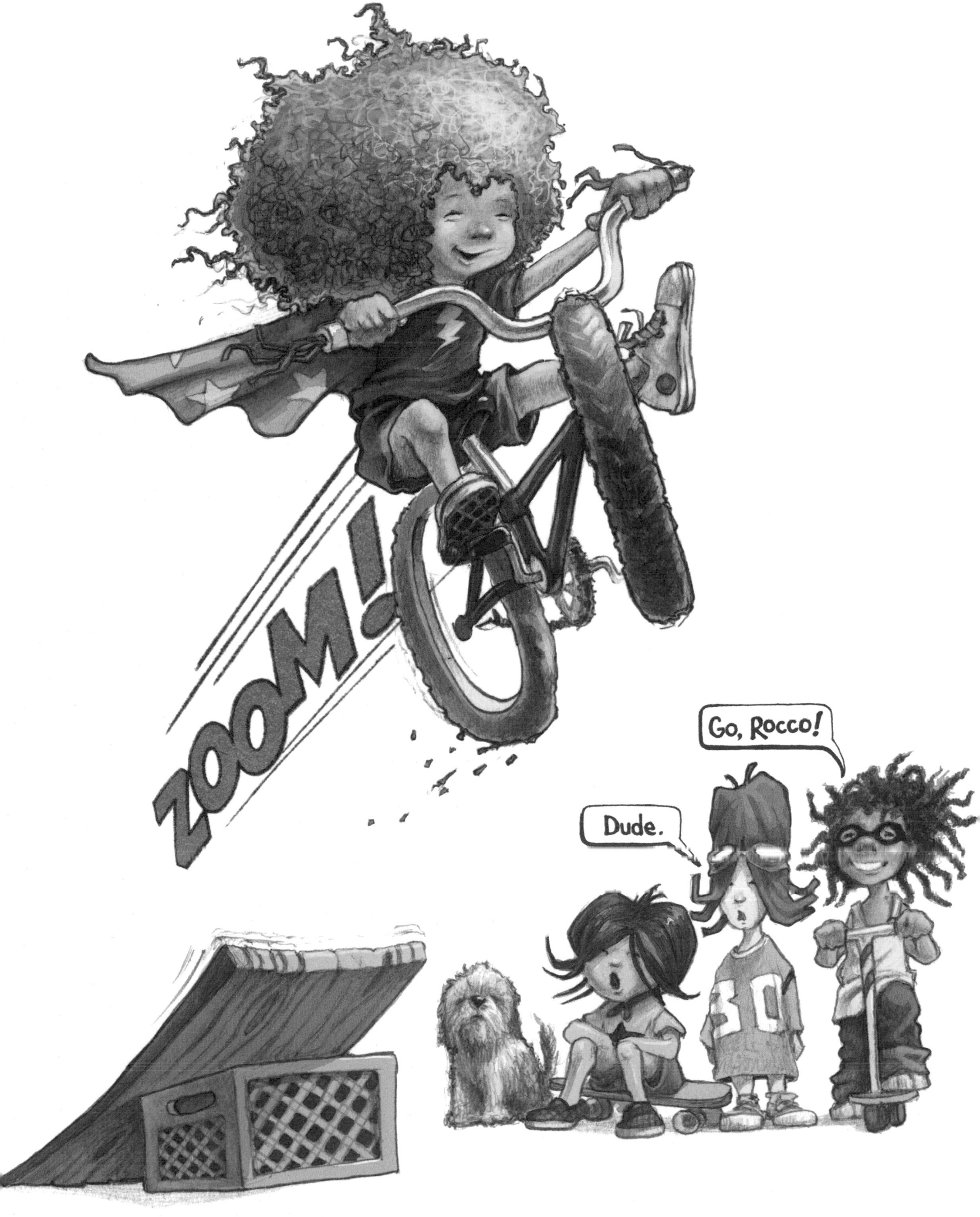
ZOOM!!
Go, Rocco!
Dude.

My **friends** had superpowers too.

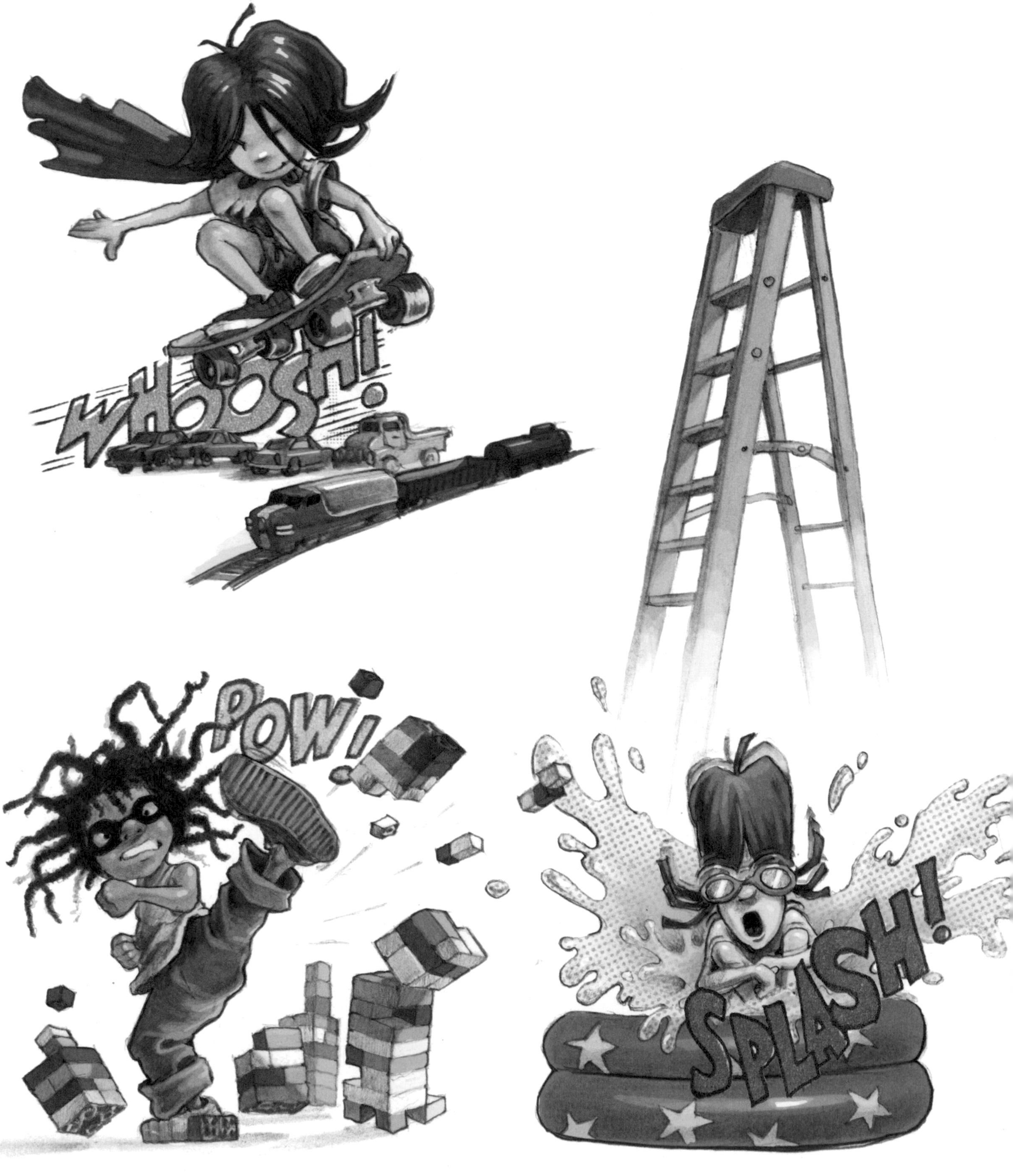
WHOOSH!
POW!
SPLASH!

And together, we were **unstoppable**!

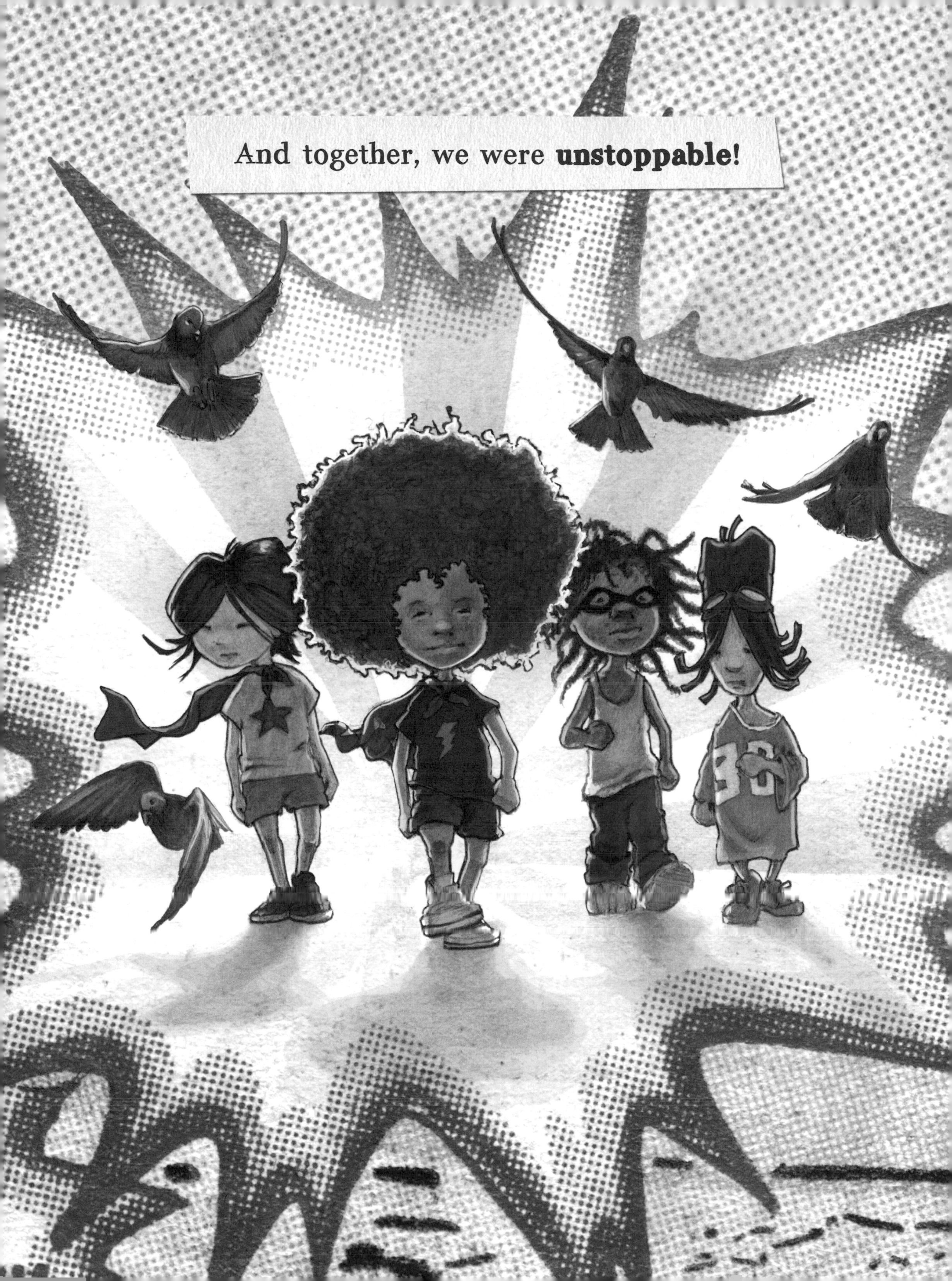

33

One day, while preparing
for our latest quest,

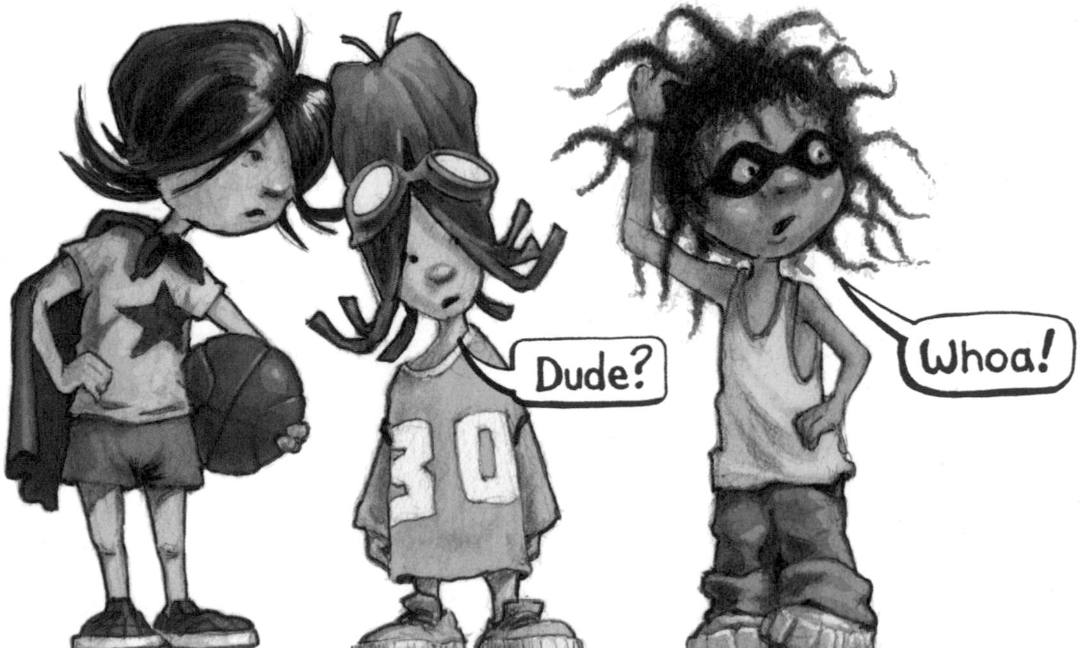
Dude?
Whoa!

I was **captured** . . .

and dragged away to the **villain's lair.**

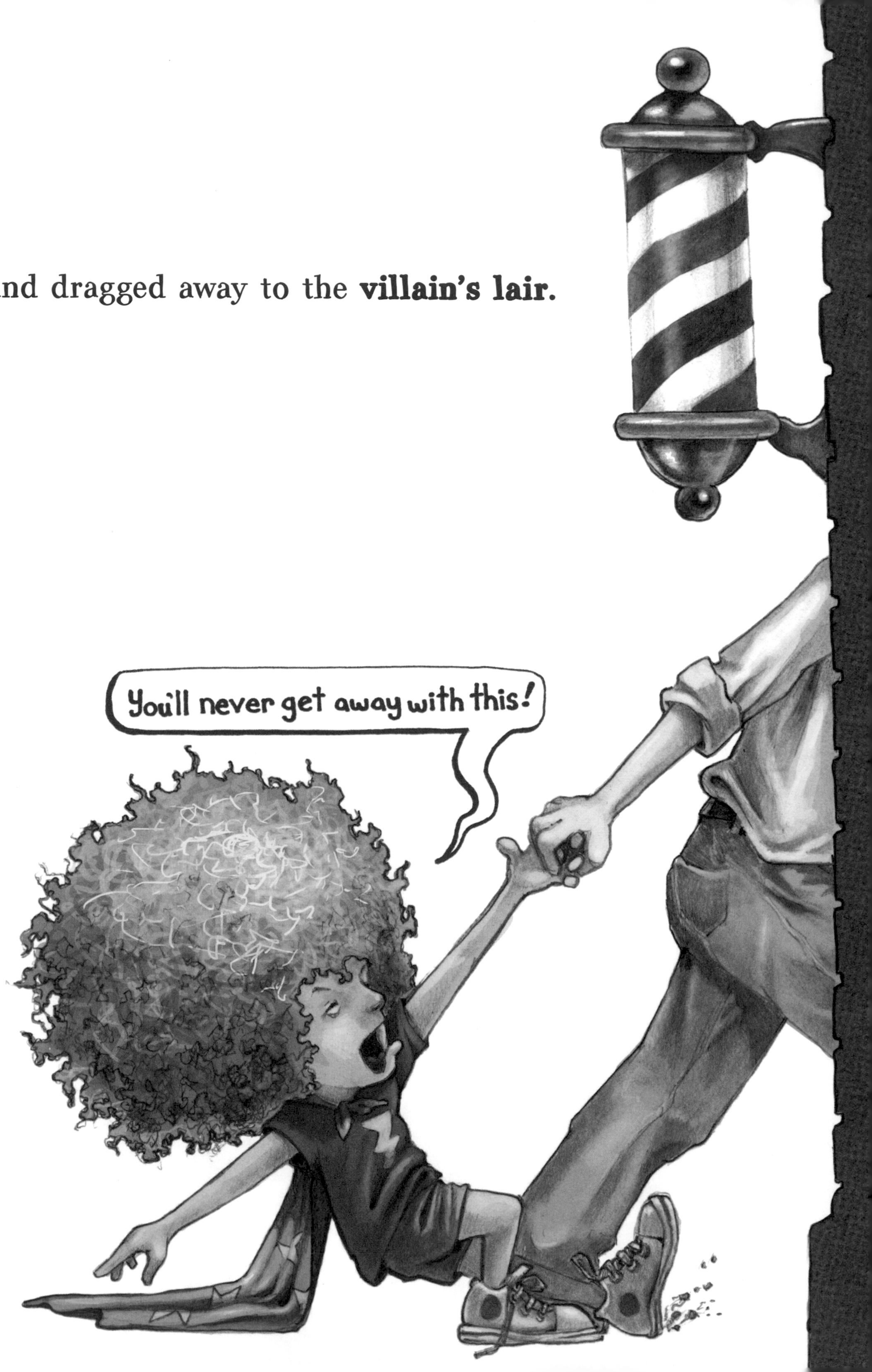
You'll never get away with this!

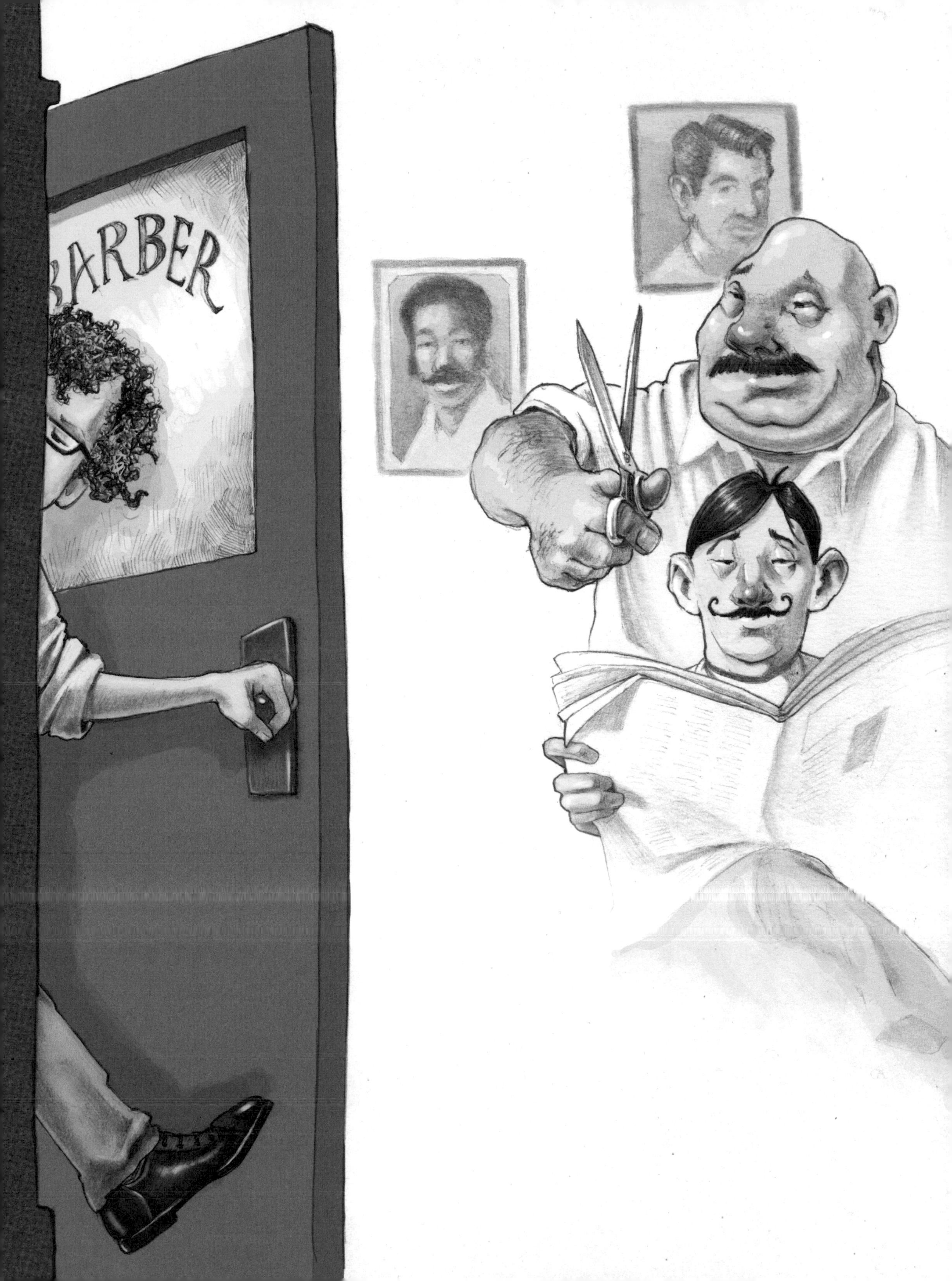
BARBER

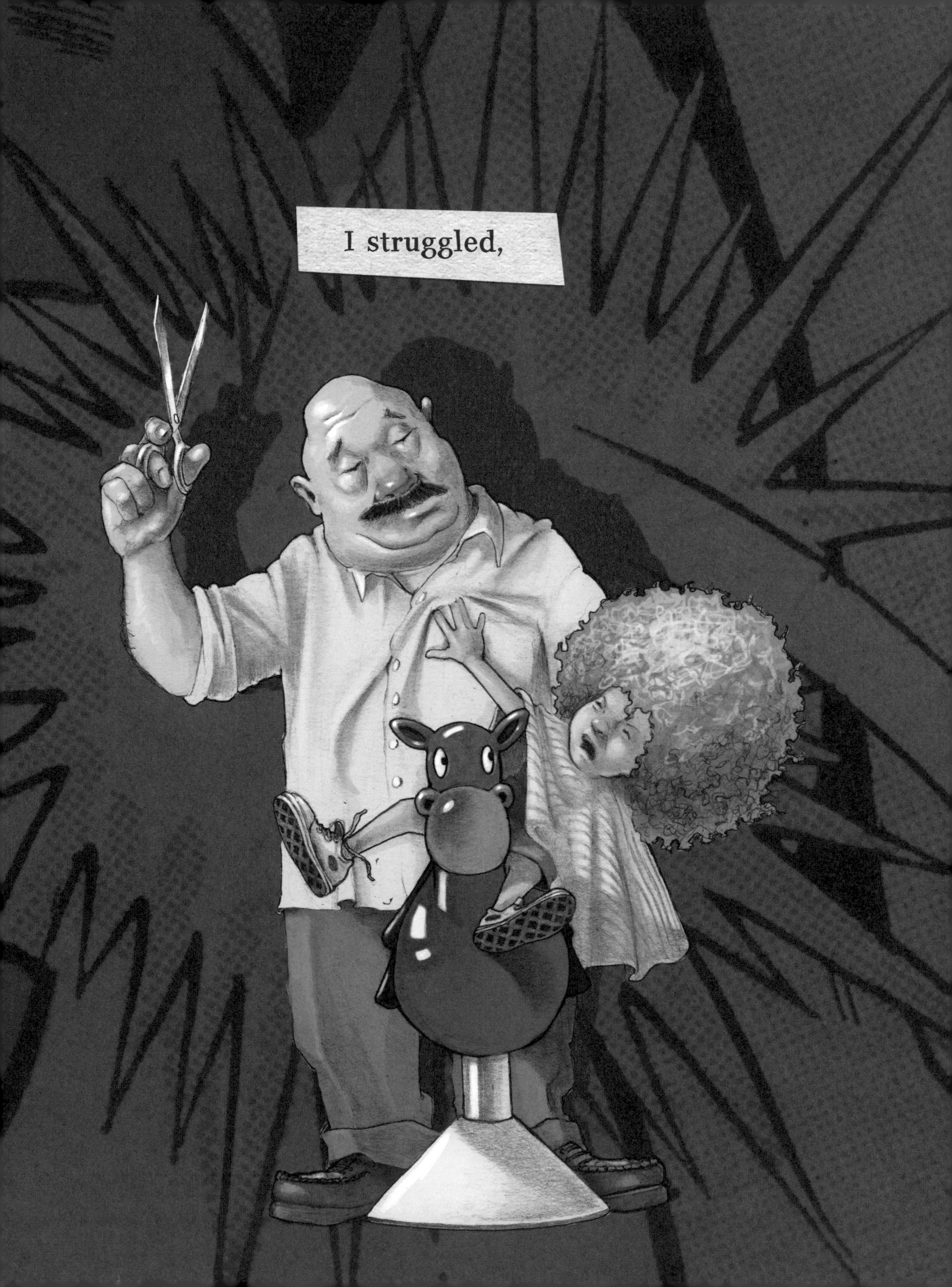
I struggled,

but the **big brute** stole my powers.

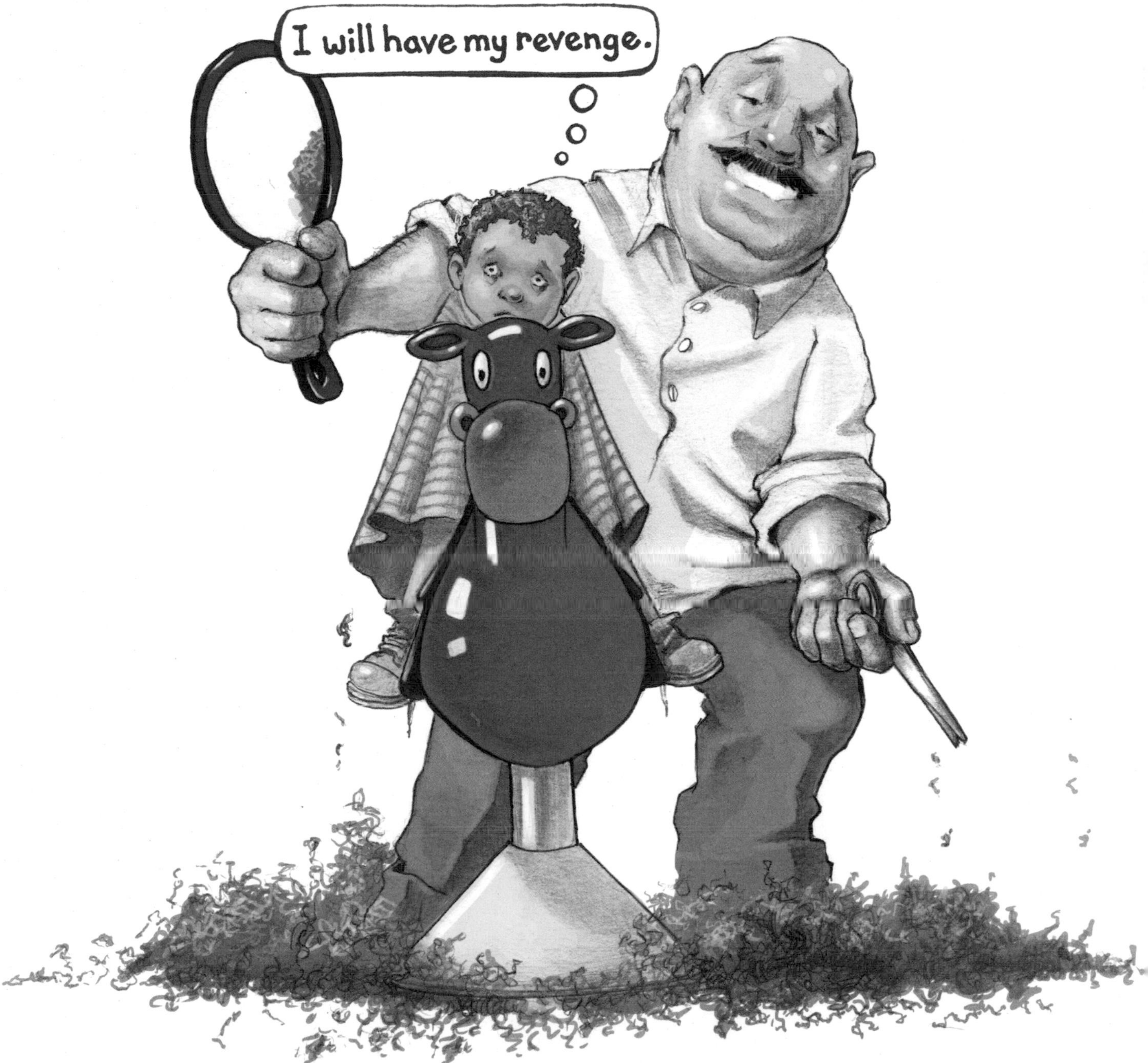
I will have my revenge.

When I finally escaped,
I could barely make it back to my
hideout.

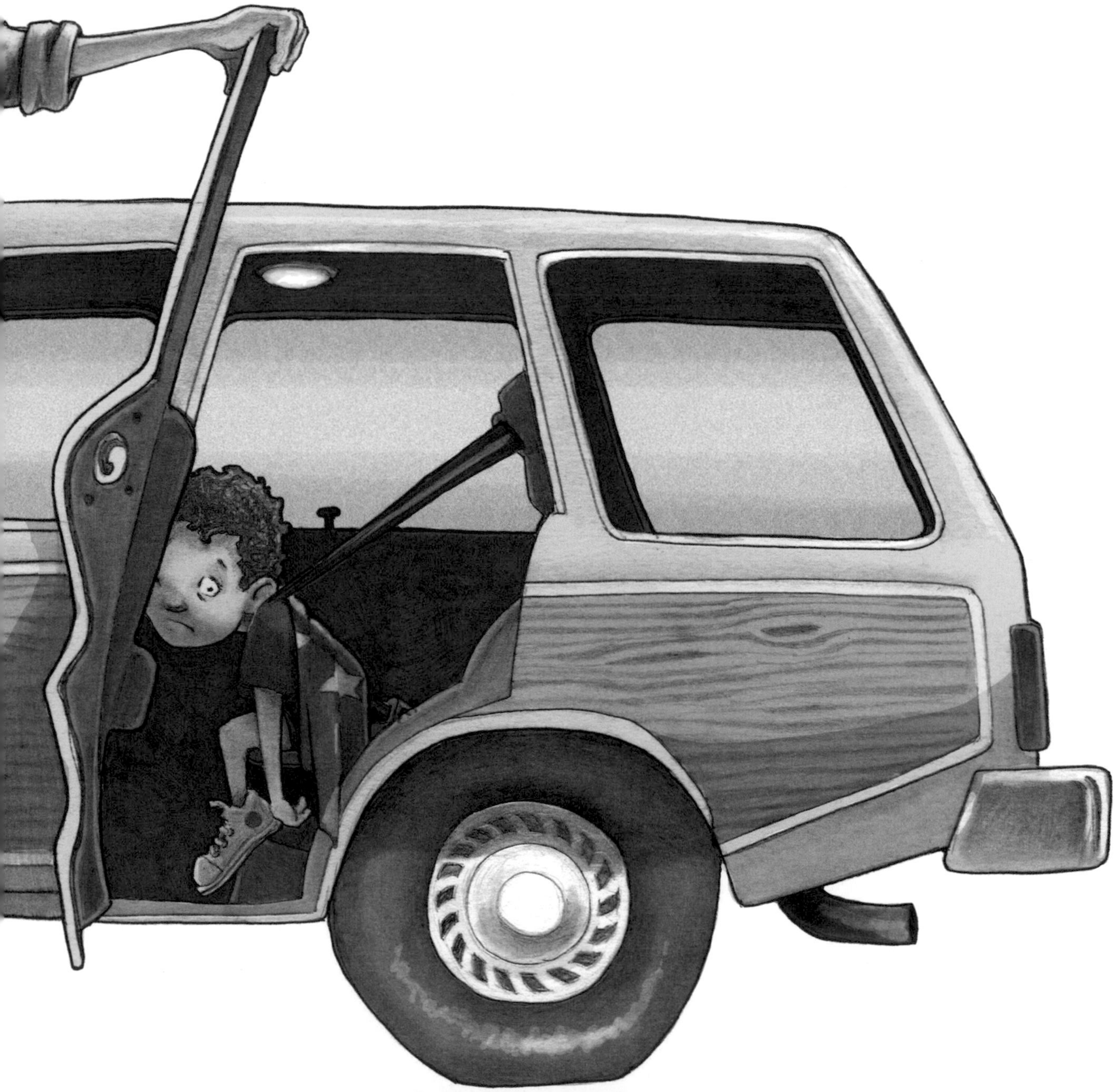

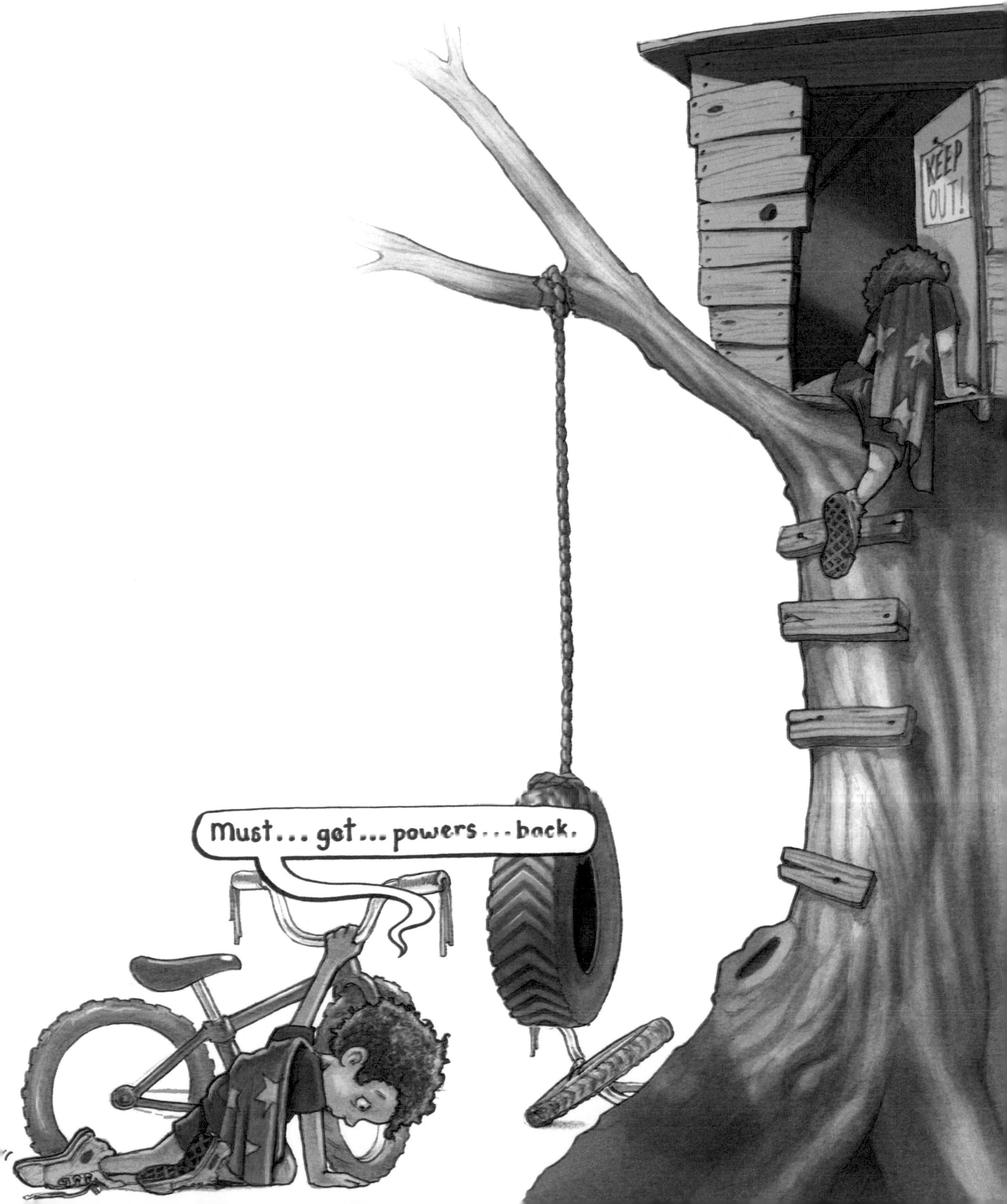
KEEP OUT!
Must... get... powers... back.

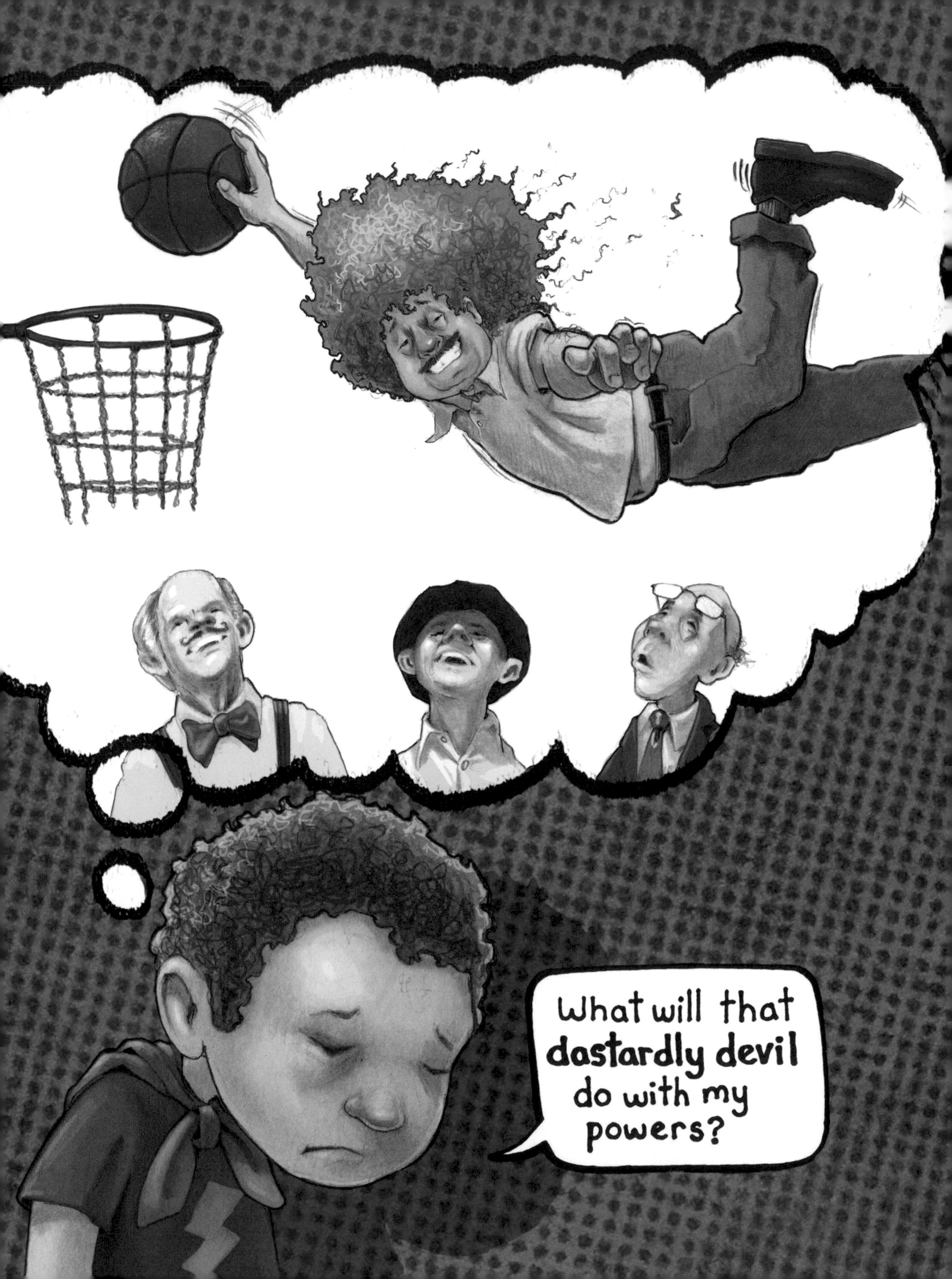
What will that **dastardly devil** do with my powers?

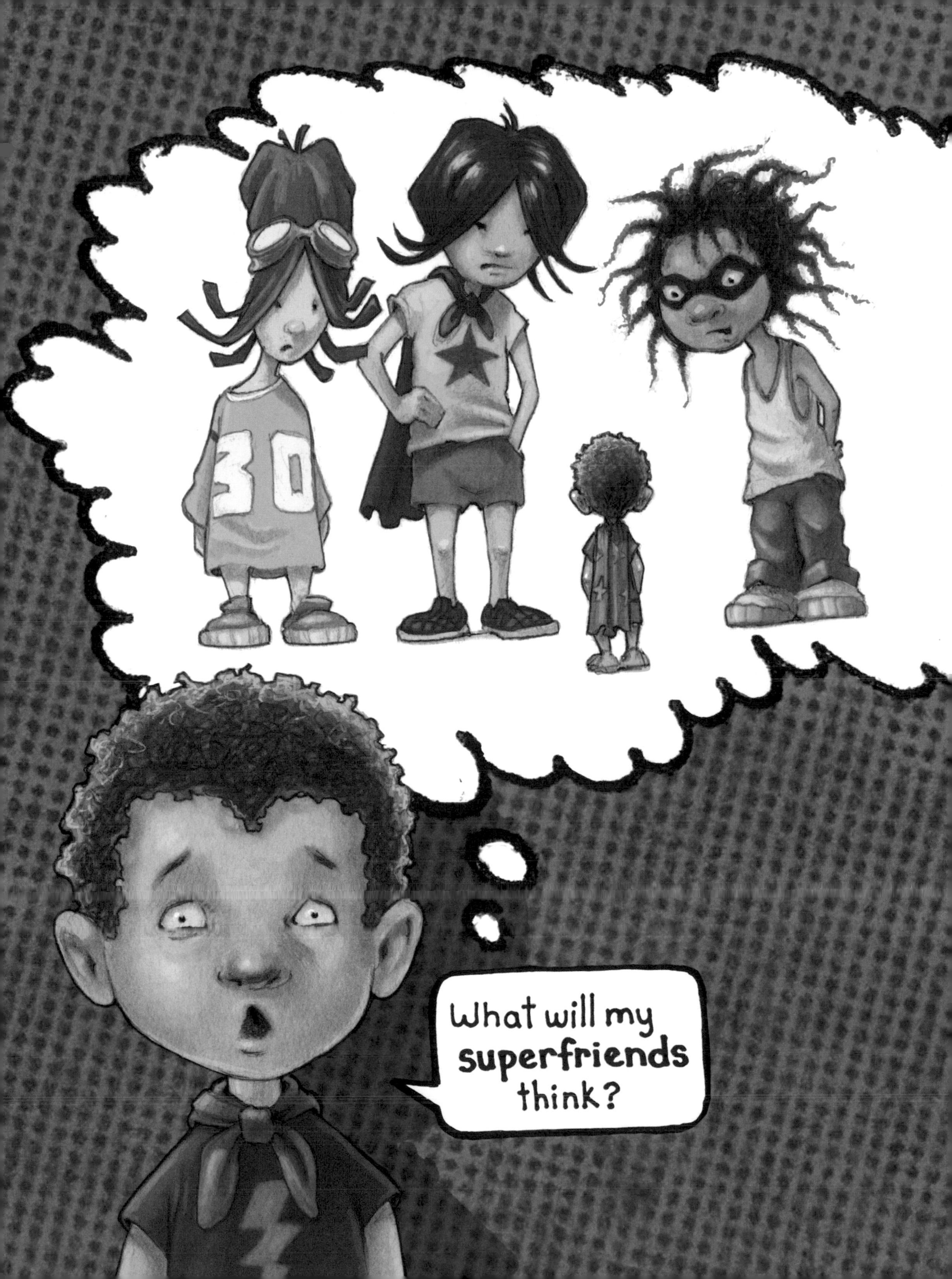
What will my superfriends think?

I tried
replacing my powers,

but nothing worked.

Not even **Sidekick Sam** could help.

Back at **headquarters,**

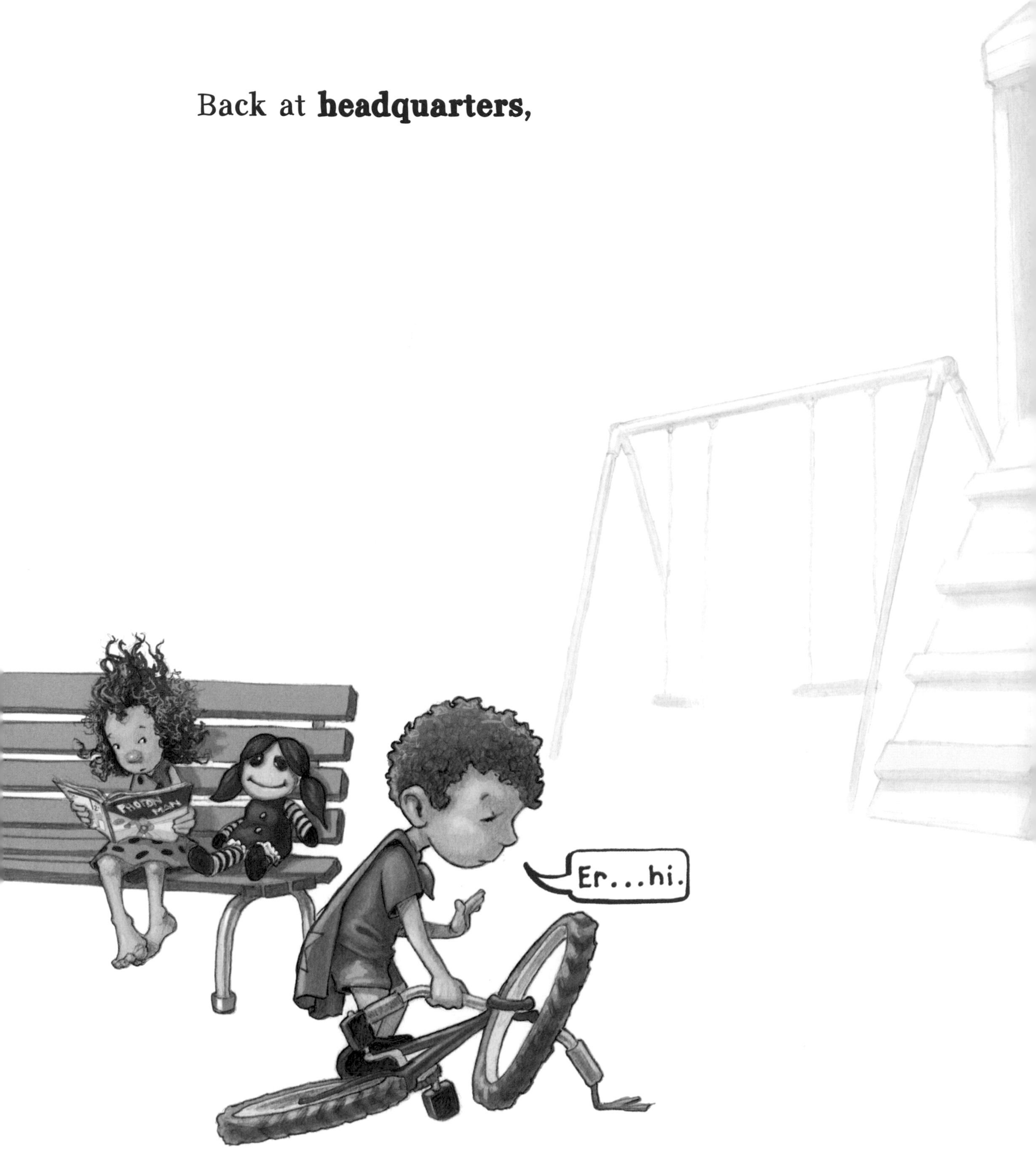
PHOTON MAN
Er...hi.

I saw that my superfriends' powers
had been stolen too.

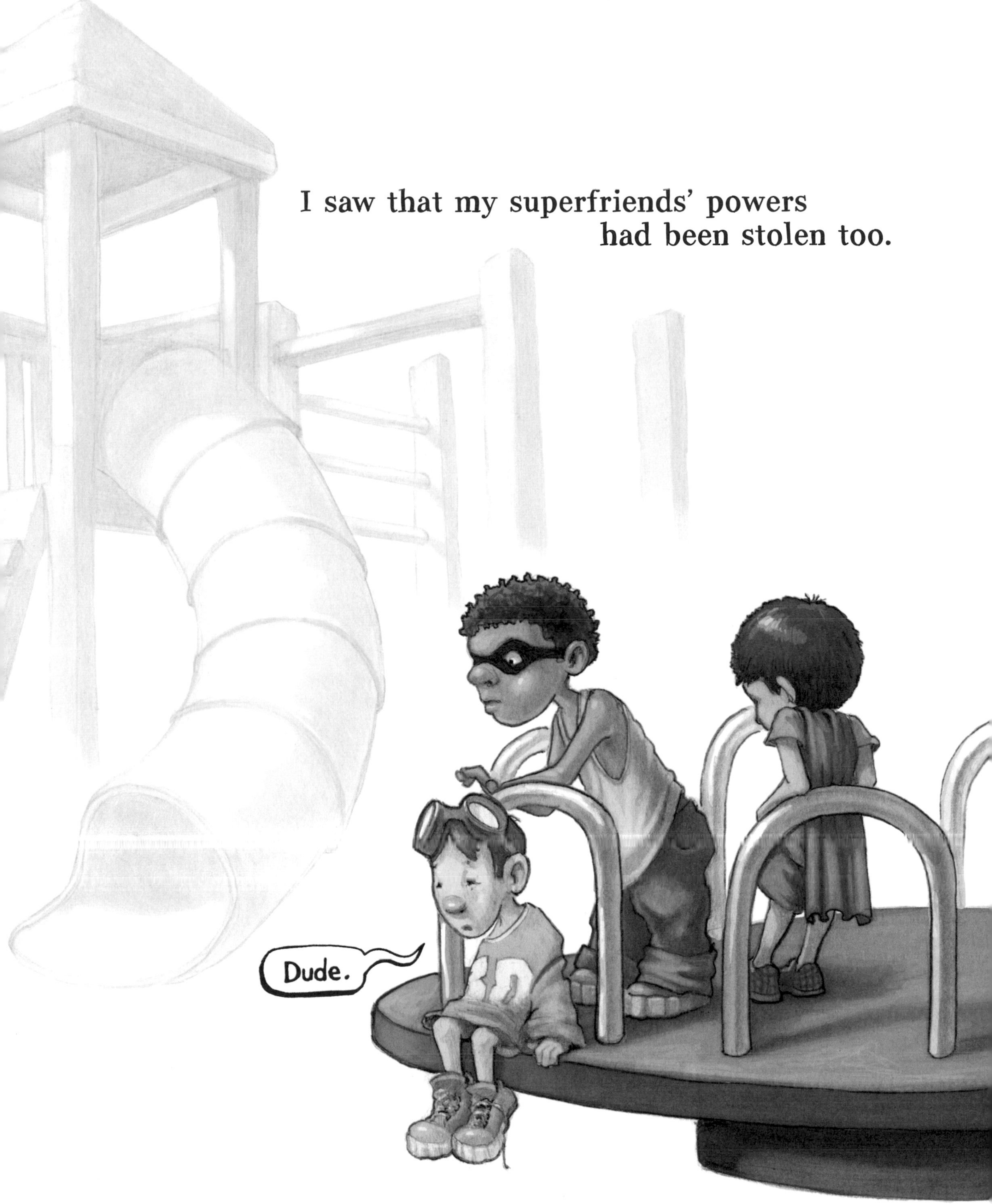
Dude.

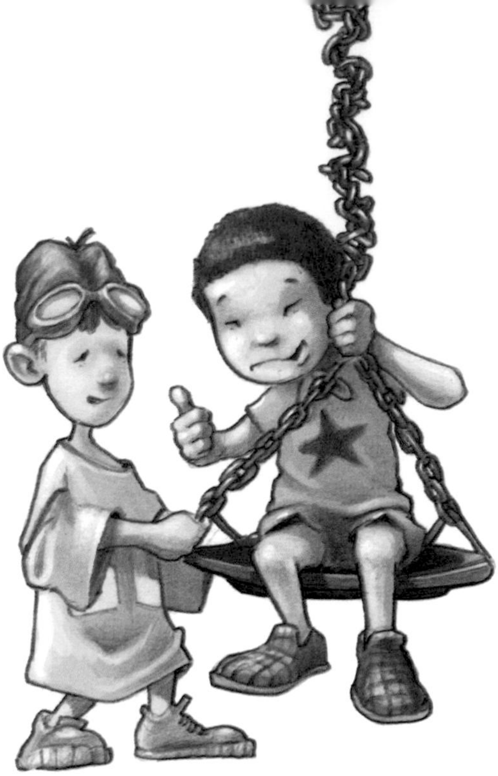

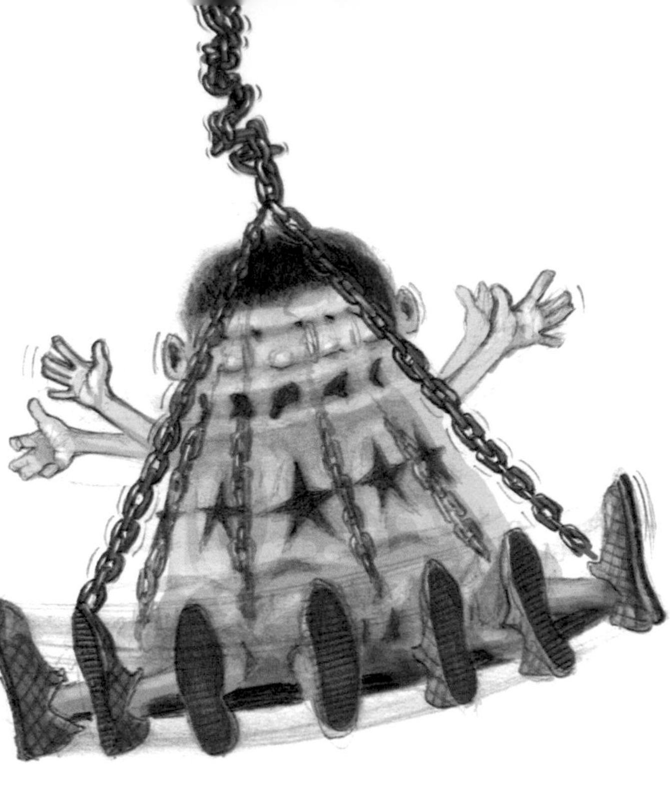

We tried everything to get back our strength,

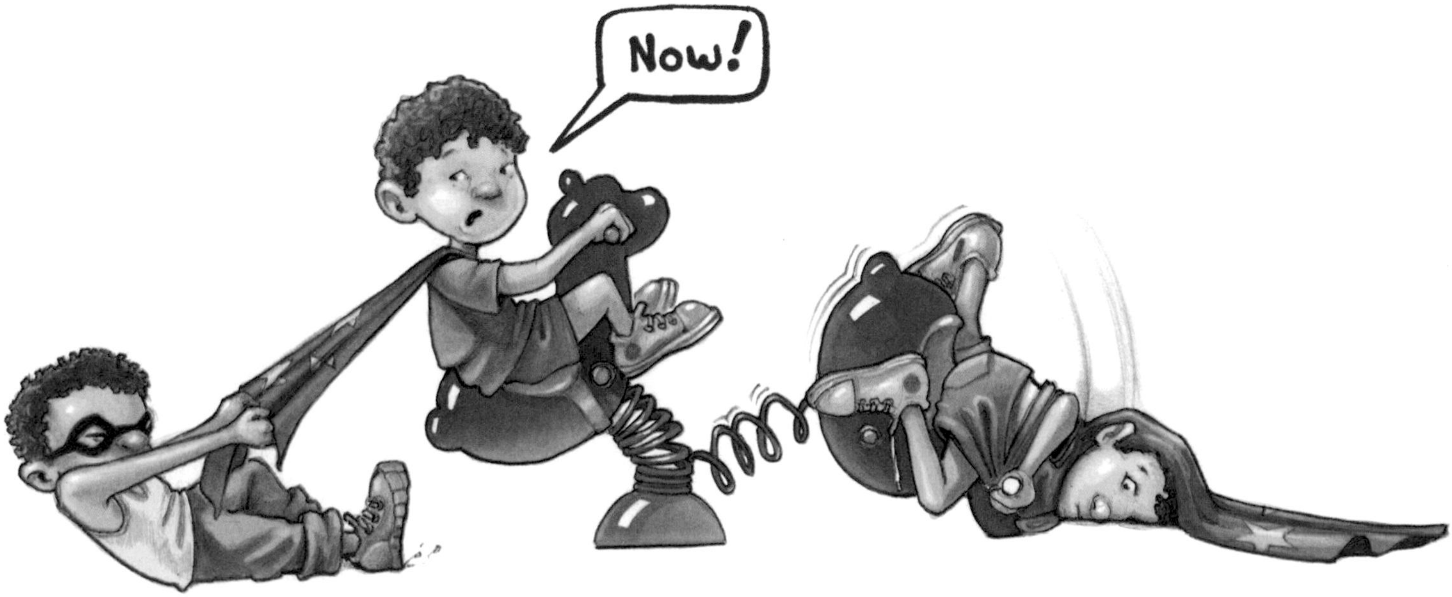
Now!

but it was useless.
We were **doomed.**

Then, suddenly,
we discovered a little hero in trouble.

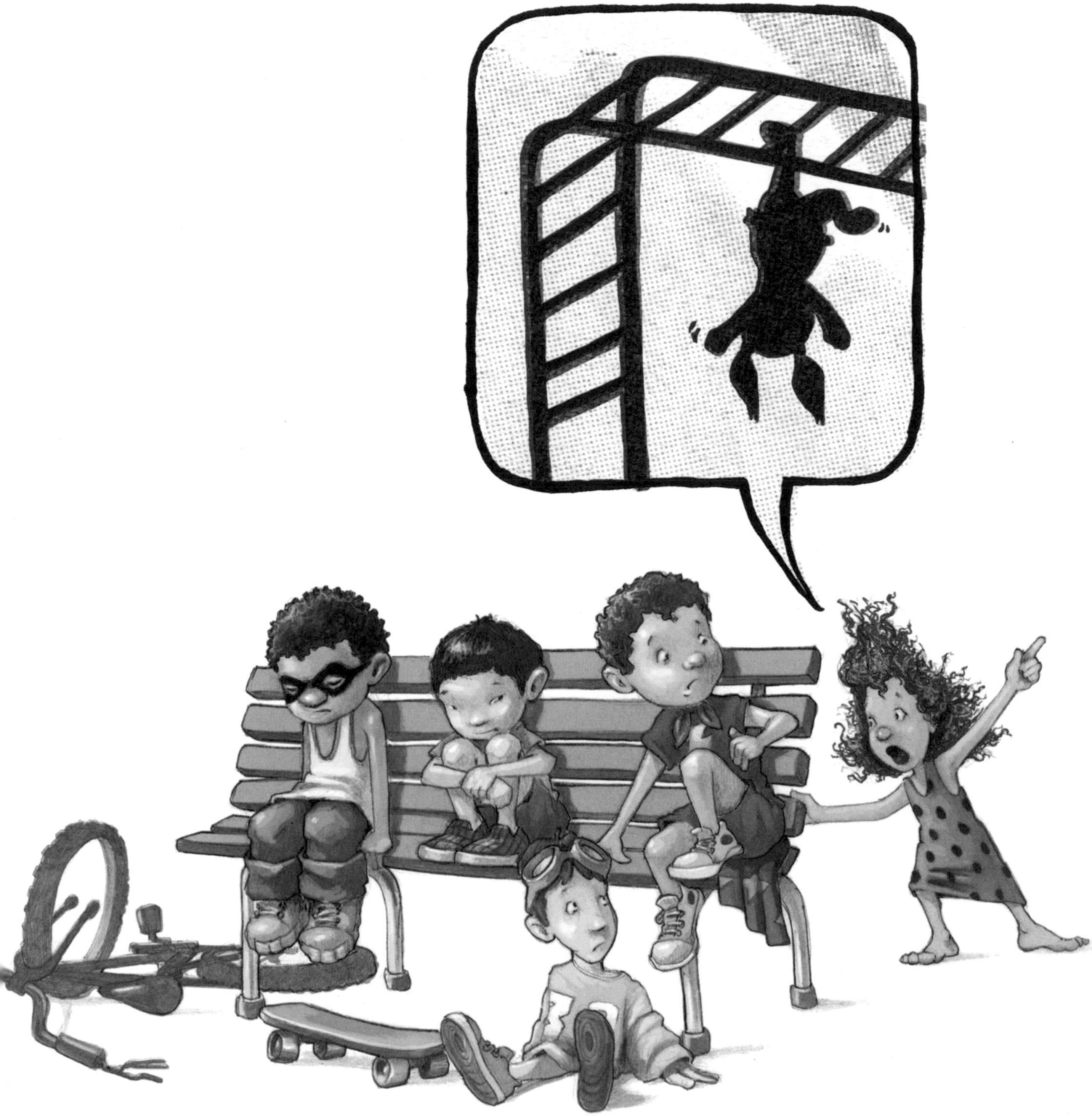

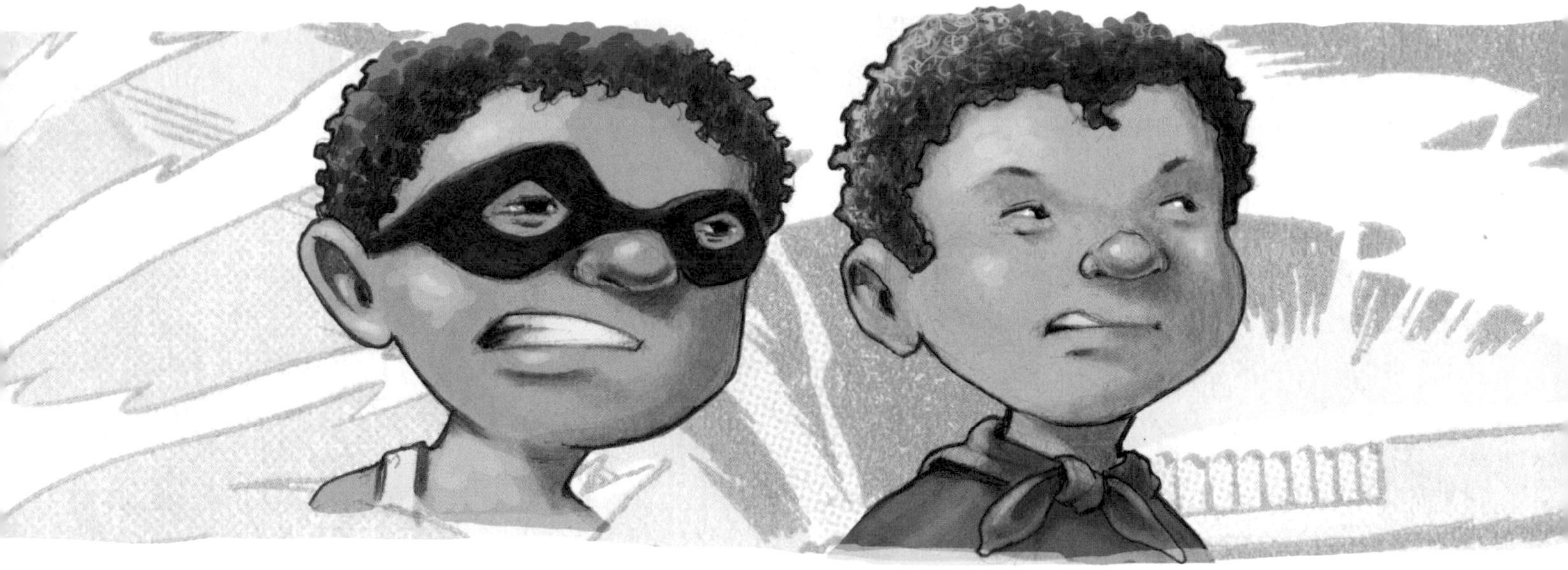

Power **surged** through us,

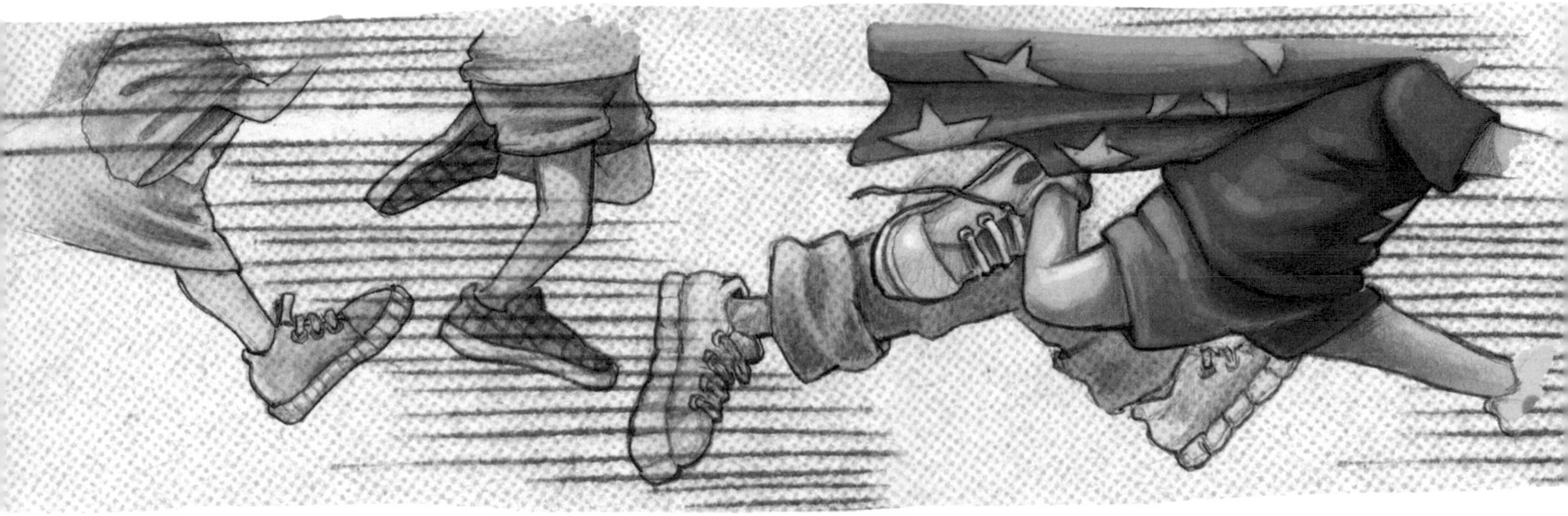

and we **sprang into action.**

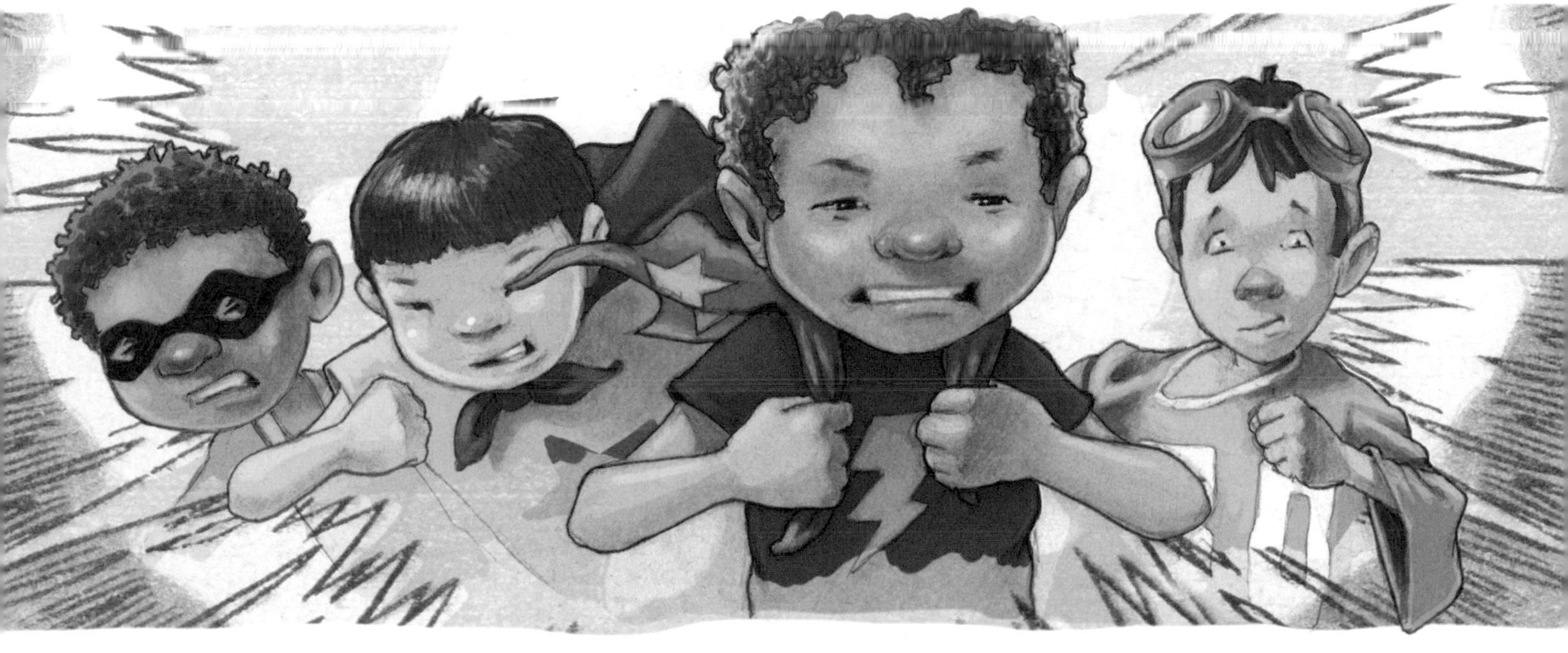

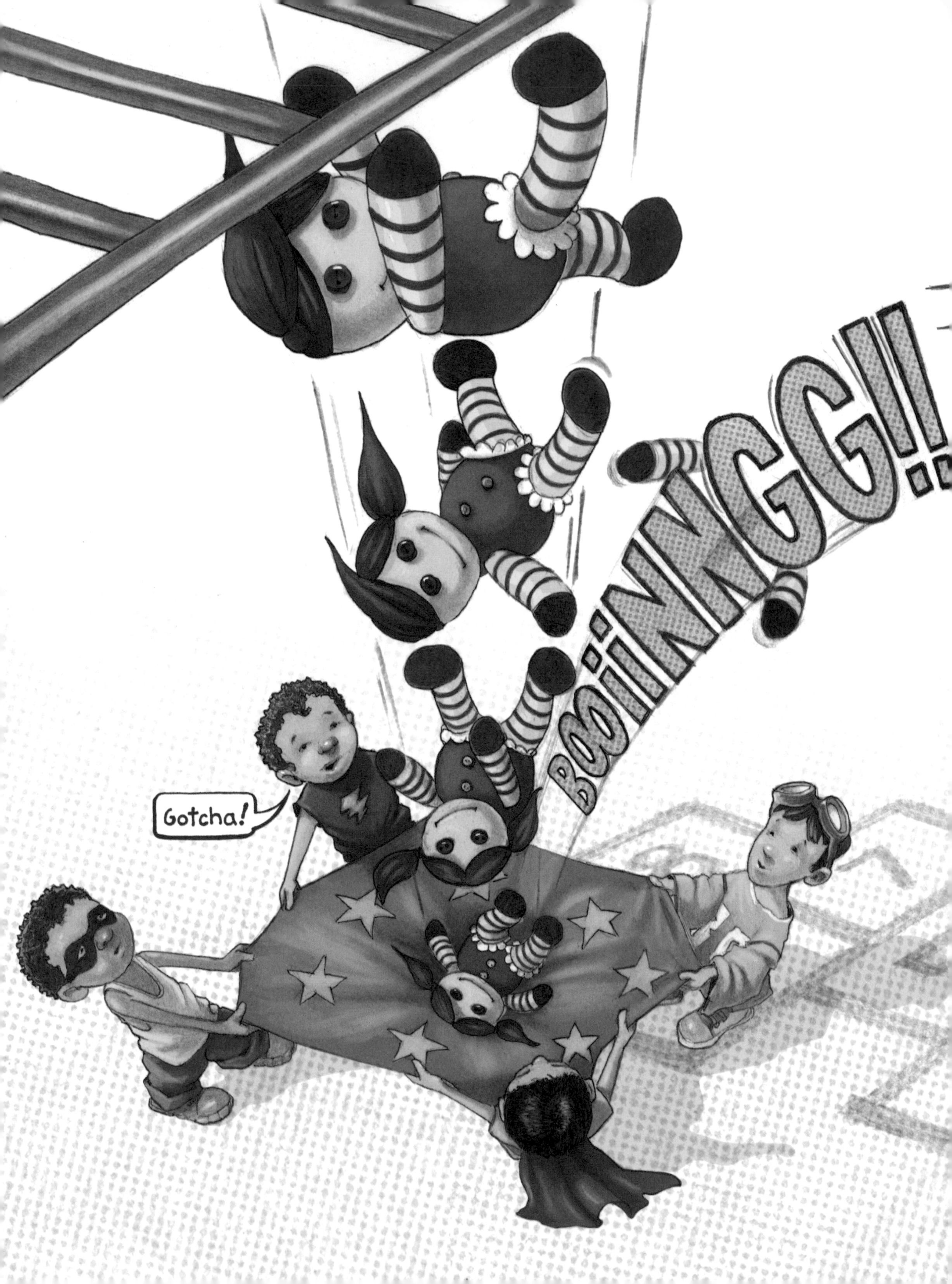
BOOiiiNNNGG!!
Gotcha!

After we saved the day,
it was **obvious** that even
without hair . . .

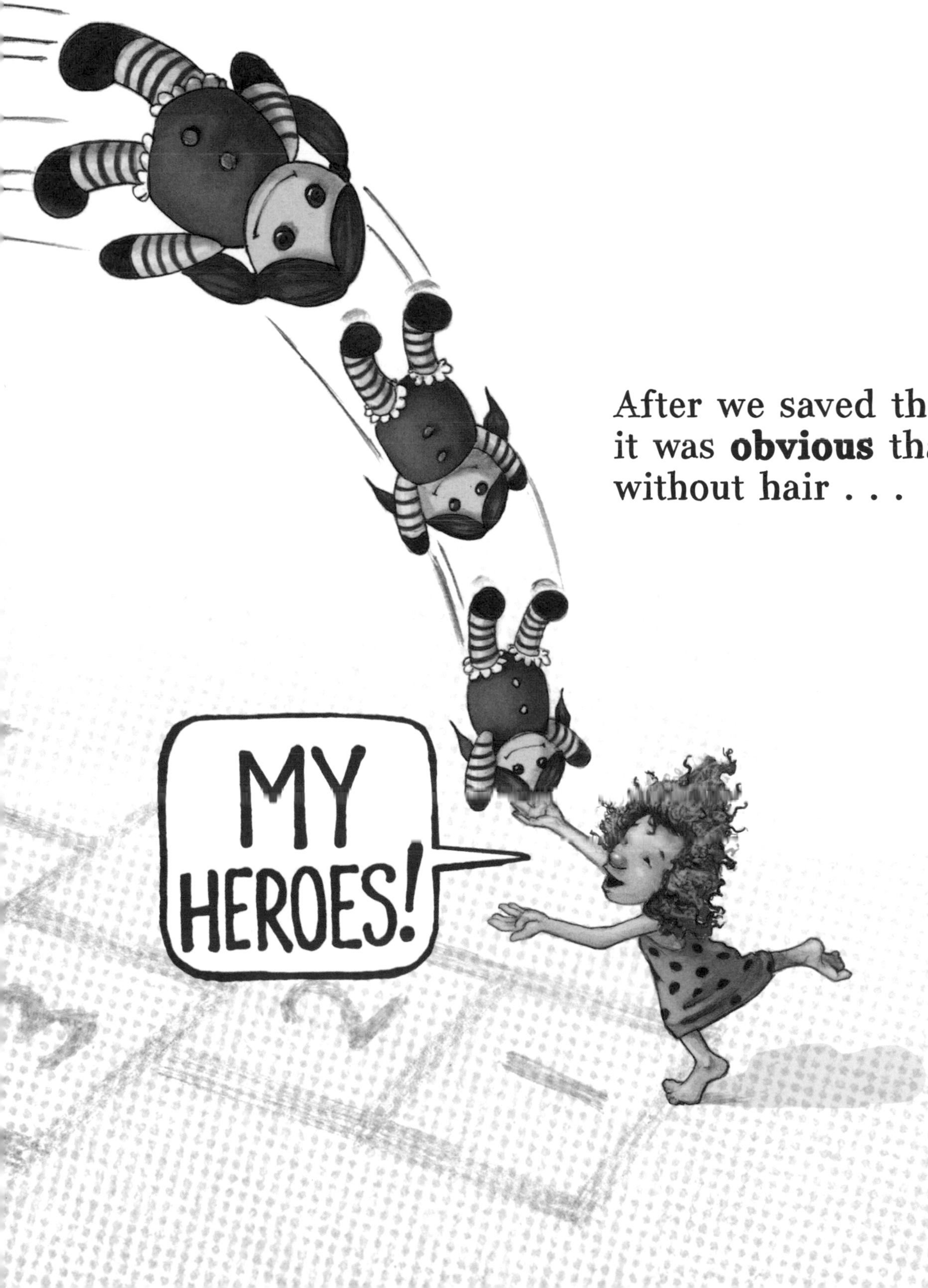
MY HEROES!

we were

STILL
SUPER!

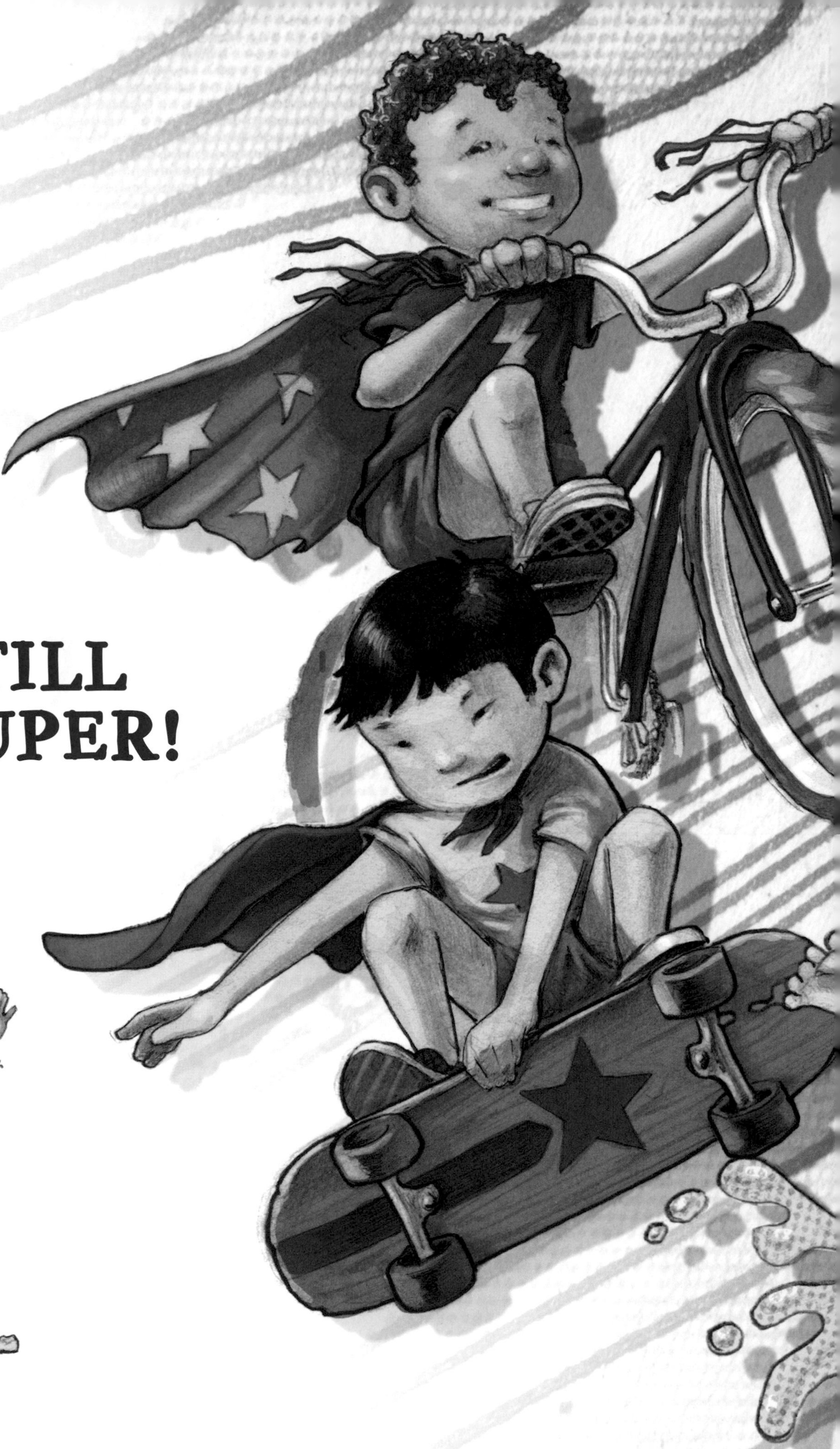

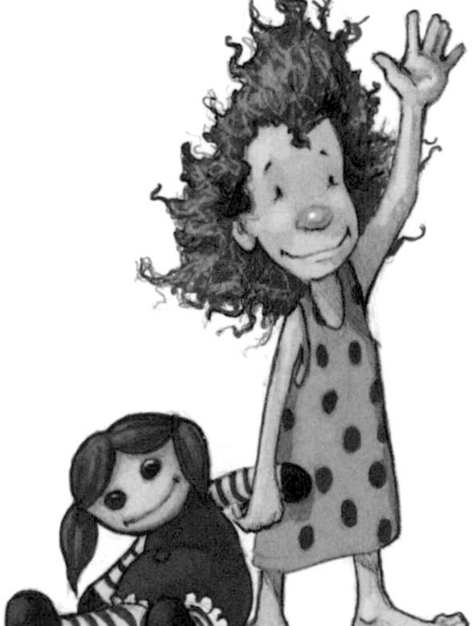

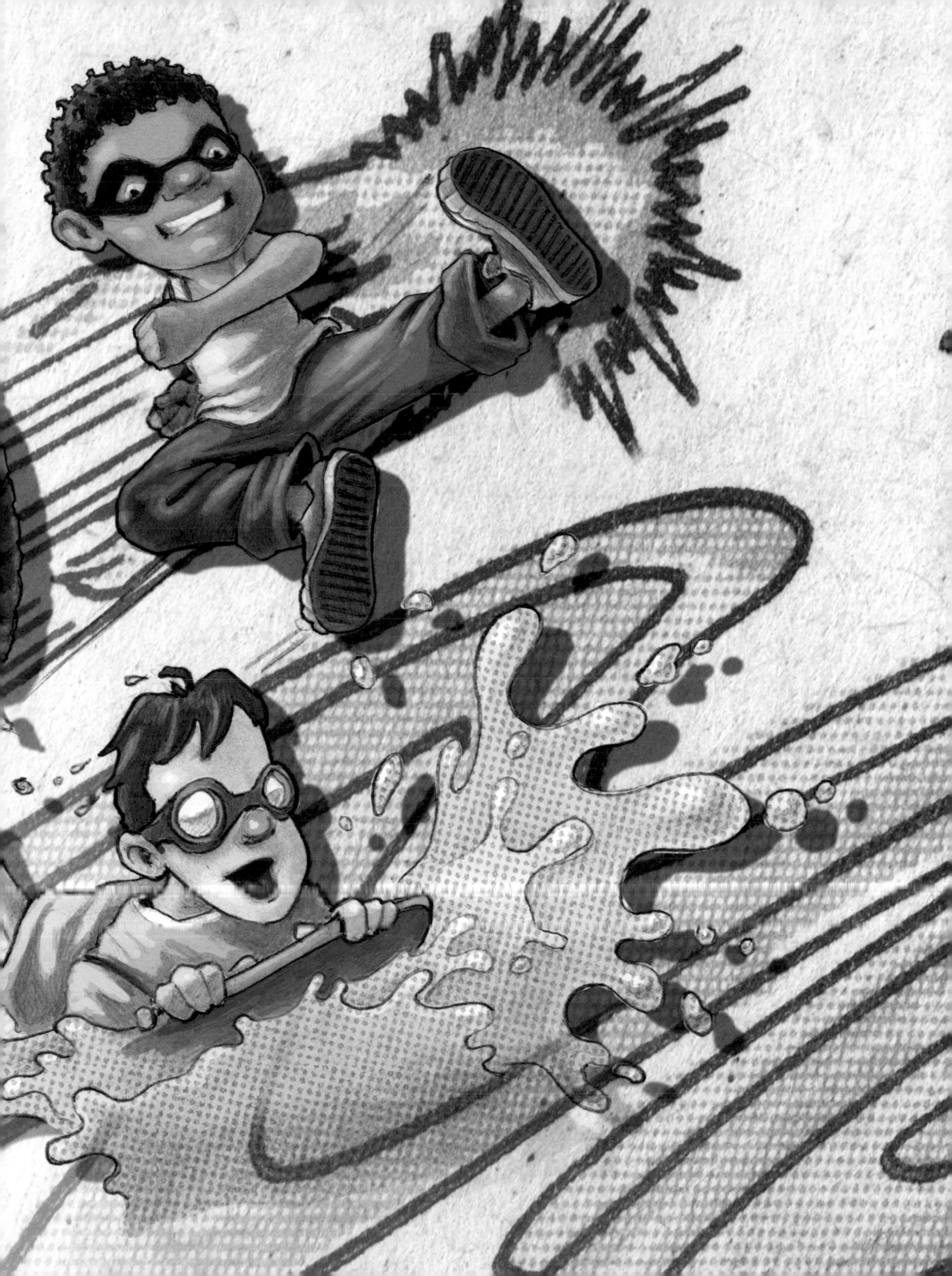

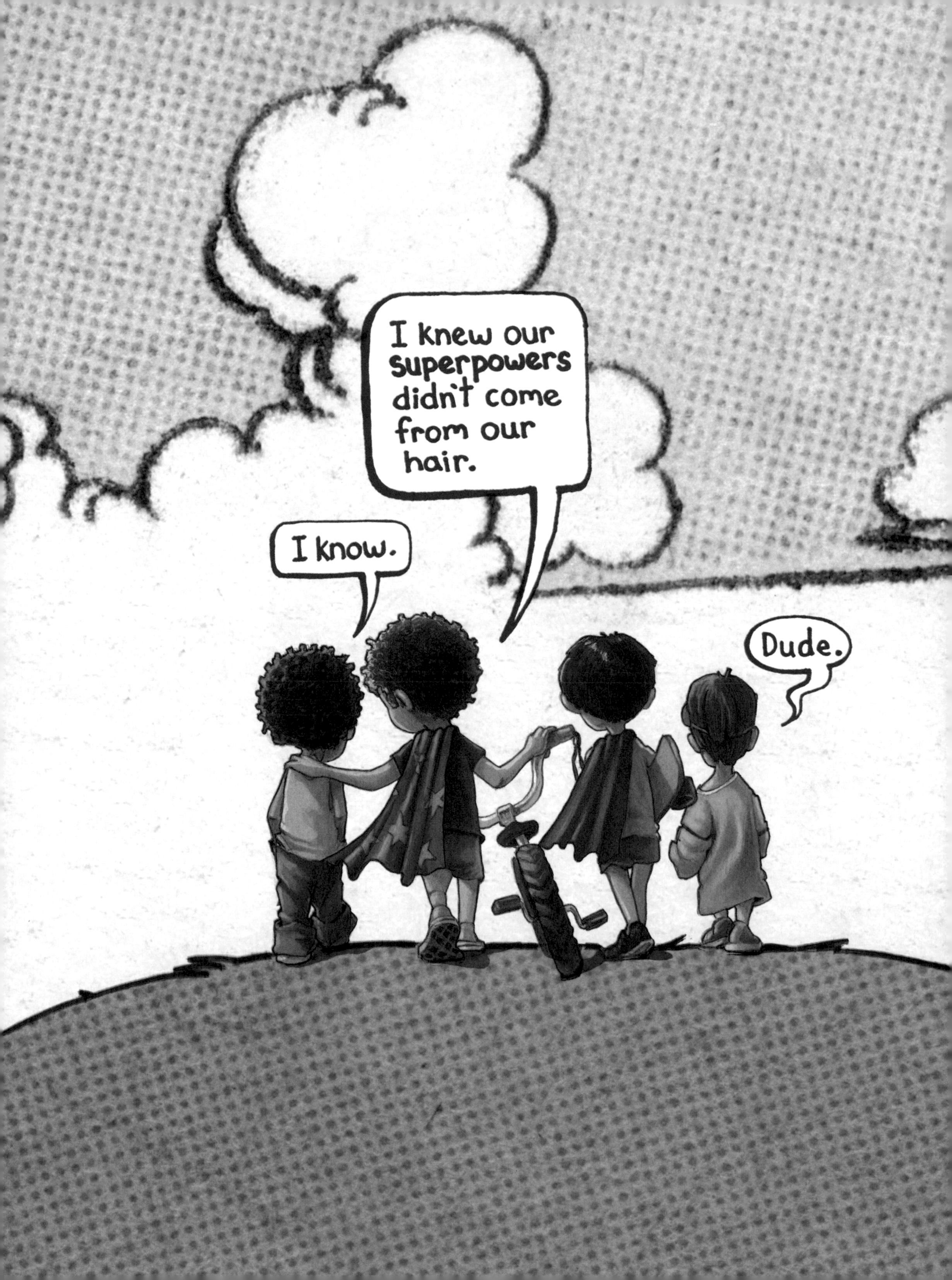
I knew our superpowers didn't come from our hair.
I know.
Dude.

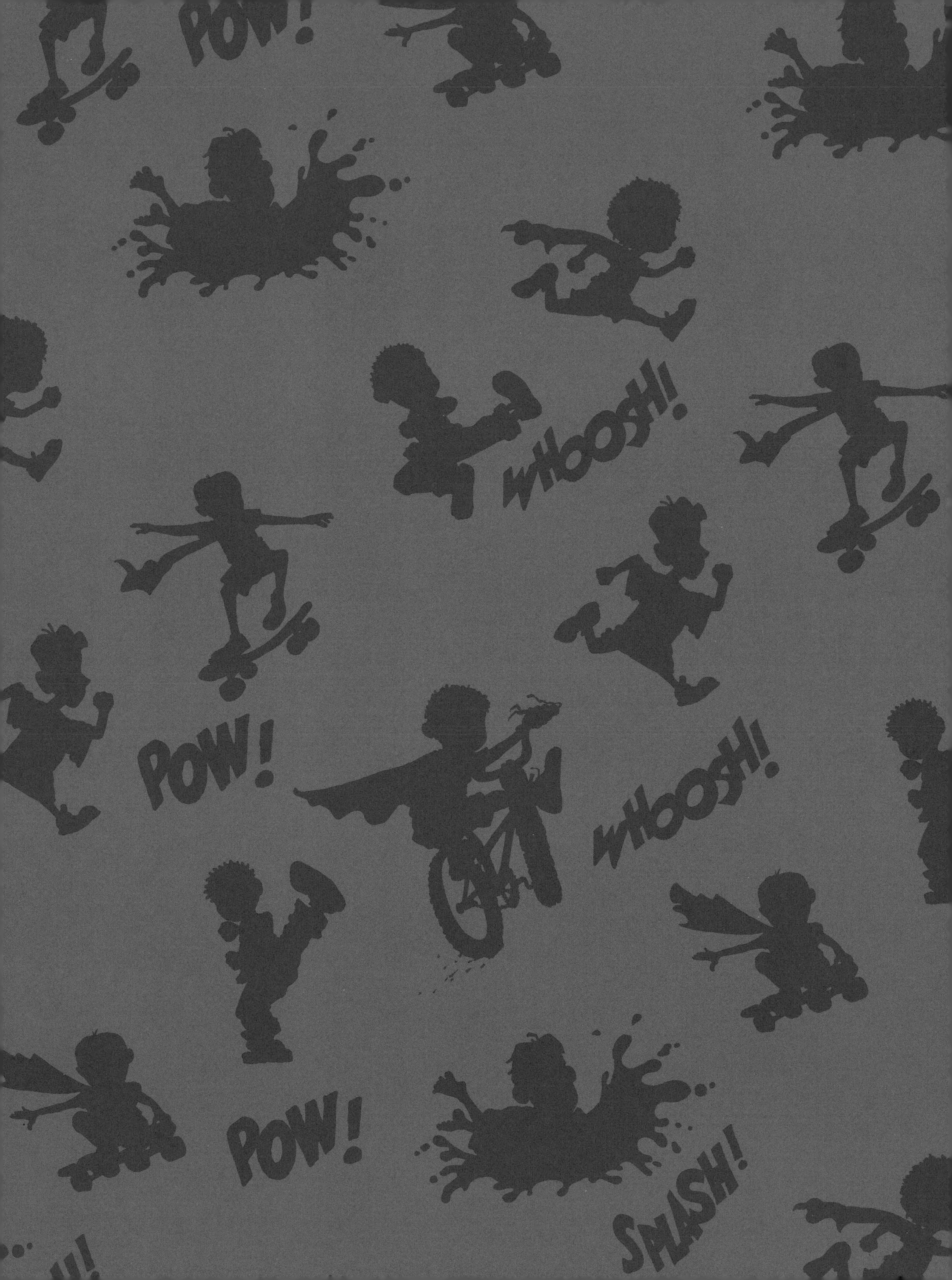
POW!
WHOOSH!
POW!
WHOOSH!
POW!
SPLASH!